Seasons of Love

Second Chances

Ramona Levacy

For That Which Must Be Tried

As always, for Mom (now in heaven) and Dad, who brought me into this world and pointed me in the right direction.

And for my husband and sister, my closest, lifelong friends who have taught me the most about forgiving and being forgiven.

Contents

Introduction

The relationship between our God and His humans lies at the heart of the Word of God. The story opens in a void from which the Creator God Almighty forms the heavens and the earth and everything else on or in it, including a man and a woman created in His image (with the ability to reflect God's essence since God Omnipotent has no form). Adam and Eve walk in the garden with God. In this perfect world, God and humans have an informal sort of relationship, like a loving parent with his children.

But then the Fall happens. Adam and Eve eat the forbidden fruit and are thrown from the Garden of Eden, out of the intimate relationship with their LORD. The rest of the Bible story involves the steps it takes to bring humans back into relationship with God again, despite all the backward steps we take in our journey toward God.

God loves us. He loves us so much, He is willing to let us choose to seek Him. When we seek, He always shows up. His ultimate act of love happened when He came to earth in the form of flawed humanity, lived a flawless life, and yet gave that life to make a way for humans to come back into relationship with God Almighty.

Through the Holy Spirit in us, we learn to lean in Jesus' direction.

We understand more fully than before the value of forgiveness. And we learn that God wants nothing less than our love, all of it, freely given to His will and the needs of the downtrodden all around us, including those poor in Spirit, who seek the earth's treasures rather than heaven's.

Thinking about how much God loves us, how patient He is, how slow to anger, I got the notion to write about second chances, the ones we should offer to others and the all-important second chance Jesus provided for us all, nailed up on that cross.

What follows are three novellas, each exploring the concept of second chances, but otherwise unconnected. In one, a couple rekindles their high school romance. Another explores two broken people who need to accept God's healing in order to commit to each other. Finally, an older couple must overcome a crisis in their marriage just in a time of their lives when they should be powerful forces for spreading God's goodness.

I hope you enjoy these stories as much as I enjoyed telling them. Read them in whatever order you like, but please read them with the concept of forgiveness in mind.

Yours in Christ,

Ramona

Seasons
of Love
Ramona Levacy
Second Chances: A Collection
of Novellas

His Last Chance

A Novella

Then Peter came up and said to him, "Lord, how often will my brother sin against me, and I forgive him? As many as seven times?" Jesus said to him, "I do not say to you seven times, but seventy times seven.
—MATTHEW 18:21-212 (ESV)

Dakota knows the first day at yet another new school will be a rough one. What with her short height and excess weight, she has always been an easy target for bullies. What she doesn't expect to find that day is a girl who will become her friend for life and a boy who will help Dakota see herself as someone of value for the very first time.

But life happens to Dakota just like everybody else. As a military kid, she can't be surprised when her dad announces yet another move too soon after Dakota settles into her best life ever. Shifting her focus to her Ivy League dreams, Dakota keeps in touch with her now long-distance friend and tries to forget her first boyfriend.

Eight years after Dakota leaves central Texas, she meets her first love for the second time. Does she have the courage to give him another chance? Or will she give in to her fear of never being enough?

The Beginning

My mother's hair fairly glows in the early morning light as she pulls to a stop one block from the high school. I turn in the passenger seat, licking my dry lips. Every time we move, which is often since my father is in the Special Forces, Mama changes her hair color. This time, she has chosen platinum blond. With her ruby-red lipstick, she looks a lot like Marilyn Monroe.

"You sure you don't want me to go in with you?" she asks, turning to look me straight in the eye.

As sometimes happens to me, her beauty strikes at something deep inside, fairly taking my breath away. I want to be her when I grow up. Instead, when I look in the mirror at my round face and chubby cheeks, my thin, straight hair and stubby nose, I know genetics makes cruel choices. The only thing positive I inherited are my baby blues, complete with thick, long lashes, a gift from Dad.

"I'll be fine," I answer her, even though we both know that is the furthest thing from the truth. Before she feels forced to say something encouraging that will only sound hollow, I pop open the door on our Hyundai SUV and practically leap to the curb. "Thanks again for bringing me," I turn to tell her. "I'll catch the bus home."

"I love you sweetheart," she tells me, her smile bright as a solar flare.

"You too," I mumble, closing the door of the SUV with more force than needed, wincing. Guilt slices through me. Mama's not responsible for our move from Hawaii to this small town in central Texas, where the flat landscape feels as blank as my life, sucking the energy from my cells like a Hoover.

Hearing Dad's voice in my head, ordering me to stand

straight and march like my life depends on it, I turn toward the school and concentrate on placing one foot in front of the other. Fear, so much of it that I can smell it on me like a cheap perfume, makes my heartbeat quicken and my palms sweat. I tug on the strap of my new backpack, a cheap, nondescript blue because somebody's sure to stuff it with open ketchup packets before the week is out.

As I round the curve, the large, brown brick building comes into view, its many windows like gaping eyes, waiting to witness my upcoming humiliation. At 5'2" and 180 lbs., I don't expect to avoid the snickers and mean pranks reserved for people just like me. I straighten my shoulders and take in a deep breath. Do I really see myself as weak? Dakota Fleming, only child of Doug and Grace Fleming, survivor of twelve moves in the past nine years, straight-A student and first chair violinist extraordinaire?

Dad's voice rings in my ears again, that saying of his that pushes me forward every time I am ready to give up. *On the battlefield, there are no second chances.* A new schoolyard when I look like this here? I can't think of a more accurate description of a battlefield.

"What do we have here?" a nasal voice sing-songs as if on cue, bringing my attention back to the smells of asphalt and teen angst hanging in the air.

I pitch my head forward and keep walking, but I feel the blush creeping up my neck, betraying me. The sidewalk beneath my feet has shifted, causing an uneven path so that I work hard at watching my step on it. The last thing I need is tripping over my own two feet. I did it once in Beverly Hills and wound up face first in a koi pond filled with prized fish.

"Wait up," a girl's voice calls. I don't stop until she adds, "please," in a kind voice with a hint of desperation to it.

The girl is tall, probably 5'8", with curly red hair and freckles covering her face and arms. She's clutching her Vera

Bradley backpack to her chest, her eyes bouncing here and there .

"You new, too?" I ask her as she comes to a quick stop beside me.

She gives a quick nod. "I'm Em, short for Emily. You look so nice. Are we supposed to dress up for the first day?" She glances down at her jeans and button-down shirt and grimaces.

I wear dresses with a high waist and skirt that flares because it helps disguise my stoutness. Em's straightforwardness makes me smile, the last thing I expected. "Em, I'm Dakota. You look fabulous. I just like dresses." I bite my lower lip, thinking how silly my choppy sentences sound.

But Em doesn't seem to notice. Instead, a new worry creases her brow. "I wonder which direction is the office?" she asks, almost as if thinking aloud.

"We could find it together?" I offer, knowing full well we'll walk into the building looking like Laurel and Hardy, one of us tall and svelte, the other pleasingly plump as Mama would say.

Em begins to talk as we head into the school, her words tumbling out of her as if she has no control over them. By the time we reach the main office, I know she has moved to live with her grandmother after her parents' divorce, that her mother joined a kind of cult and now teaches yoga and meditates with the trees, while her father tours the state in a beat-up VW van playing gigs with his country band.

The school office smells like copier ink and some flowery scent I would bet belongs to the older lady in the corner, with her beehive hairdo and cat-eye shaped glasses hanging from a cord around her neck. Em and I walk up to the counter and wait. The younger secretary, a woman in her thirties wearing a school t-shirt with a jean skirt, walks up to greet us, a wide smile on her face.

"You must be our new students," she beams, glancing between the two of us. I appreciate the way she catches my eyes and keeps them instead of glancing down my body with that look, the one shuddered in disappointment that most kind people give me, unable to help themselves.

"Emily Collins, ma'am," Em says first, handing the woman a folder from the recesses of her heavy bag.

By the time the secretary has taken her papers, I have mine pulled out and ready, too. "Dakota Fleming," I tell her.

"I'm Mrs. Hardy," she says, arranging our papers. "I take care of the underclassmen. Mrs. Smith is in charge of all the rest." She glances up from the papers in front of her. "I see you're eligible for our honors classes, Ms. Fleming. I assume that's what you want."

Em shifts, making more distance between us. I bite my lower lip. I want to attend a strong university, maybe even go Ivy League, so I can't let anything, not even potential friendship, stand in the way of my goals. "Yes, ma'am," I tell Mrs. Hardy.

Within a few moments, we have our schedules. Thinking we may be good for each other, Mrs. Hardy makes sure we share homeroom and lunch. We even share orchestra, though Em plays saxophone and doubles by marching in the band. Mrs. Hardy finishes with us just in time to send us off to Rm. 211 for homeroom.

"I've never seen so many people at once before," Em breathes out as we step into the crowded corridors. She looks over at me and grins. "I must sound like the worst kind of hayseed to you."

"I think you sound like yourself, which is pretty special if you ask me," I assure her. Have I really found a friend on the first day of school? It certainly feels that way.

We reach Rm. 211 only to find our entrance blocked by a huge bulk of a boy-man. I would swear his shoulders span the width of the doorway if I didn't know better. He slouches against the jamb, the obvious muscles under his football jersey relaxed, his feet, encased in Ropers, crossed at the ankle. All we can see is the back of his blond head, the hair thick and conservatively cut.

We stand like mannequins, waiting for a clear path into our classroom. After a few moments, Em elbows me, raising an eyebrow in question. Gathering my courage, I straighten my skirt and step forward, feeling Em's hand on my back for support. The warmth of her fingers makes me smile, giving me the encouragement I need. Reaching out tentative fingers, I lightly poke the guy near his elbow. He ignores me. I turn to look at Em, feeling the flush across my cheeks. She nods hopefully, encouraging me to try again.

Clearing my throat, which suddenly feels rusty, I manage to call out. "Excuse me."

The only thing he moves are his eyes, gorgeous, amber orbs that cut to the side, assessing me head-to-toe, from my straight hair hanging down past my shoulders to the Converse tennis shoes I wear.

"Is she for real?" he asks himself. He turns back to the person he's talking to inside the room. "Daniel, looks like you're going to have homeroom with a dwarf."

Now, even my neck flames red, especially as a raucous chorus of laughter wafts into the hallway.

"Lucas Bell," a teacher's voice snaps, and the big guy waits five beats, then ten, before turning in her direction. "Get to your own homeroom now. I'm sure your little brother will be just fine on his own."

Lucas, who's probably the football captain and thinks the whole school will bow at his feet, finally pushes away from the doorframe. He nods to his brother, Daniel, before heading back down the hall, his forearm brushing against my shoulder as he passes, sending traitorous shivers up and down my spine.

I turn beside me and look up to Em. "I suppose we have to go in there now," I say, laughing as if my heart isn't cracking just that little bit more inside me.

"I can walk in ahead," Em offers.

I shake my head and square my shoulders. "No, thanks," I tell her. "Sometimes, you just have to rip off the band-aid."

A boy steps into the hallway. He's at least 6 feet and still growing, with beautiful, auburn hair and deep, brown eyes. "I'm sorry about my brother," he tells us. "He th-thinks he's super because he plays f-football."

His slight stutter makes him instantly endearing to me, but I'm completely won over when he bows slightly, offering me his elbow. "I d-dare them to laugh at you," he says.

Em falls in step behind us. I feel her breath across the top of my head, rapid and hot, as we walk into the classroom, knowing my breath comes in and out of me with the same erratic rhythm. I squeeze Daniel's arm until the poor guy winces. I hear a snort from the back of the room, but luckily Daniel's body hides me from open view.

After leading me to the first seat in the last row, Daniel waits until Em sits in the seat across from me before sliding into the desk behind me. After homeroom, I'm sure to be called dwarf, or Sleepy, or Dopey at least ten times today and maybe forever, but for this moment, I cocoon myself in a shell, concentrating on opening my notebook and doodling around the margins while the bell rings and the classroom settles down for morning announcements.

Mrs. Smart looks like she has taught for twenty or more years, standing in front of us with a tired sloop to her thin shoulders. She pushes her glasses up her nose and silences the class with one finger wave. Moving her eyes over the classroom, she glances down at the paper in her hand and sighs out, folding the announcements in her fist and tucking her arms across her body.

"Welcome to high school," she says, her voice sounding

as tired as she looks. "You're young adults now, which means I will respect your ability to make wise choices concerning your behavior unless and until you prove otherwise to me. Pay attention to the following."

As if on cue, the speakers in the corners of the room crackle, and a clipped voice begins to make announcements about club sign-ups, a pep rally, and the offerings for lunch. I study my schedule, feeling the heat of stares that may or may not be directed toward my back. I can't wait until the final period, when I have orchestra. Music calms and fills me. When I'm playing my violin, I forget about my weight, my Dad's disappointment in me, my fears of being alone.

Mrs. Smart begins roll call when the intercom ends. She wants each of us to tell the class something interesting about ourselves. Em tells everyone she spent the summer helping her grandmother can blackberries from thick vines in the woods behind their house. Daniel says he likes to ride horses, a short, direct answer that I assume helps him avoid his stutter. When it's my turn, I stand like the others, pushing my hands down the fabric of my skirt, knowing no one will believe what I am about to say.

"I can hold my breath underwater for more than two minutes."

Somebody coughs out a negative comment. Otherwise, the rest of the class seems to absorb this information just as they've listened to everyone else, with no interest whatsoever. Thankfully, the bell rings, sending us to our first period class.

Daniel stands up between me and Em. "D-do you have A lunch?" he asks.

"We do," Em answers, glancing at me as I nod in agreement to her obvious question. "We can all eat together," she finishes.

His shoulders relax, and a smile brightens his

countenance, making him something beyond handsome. For one crazy moment, I feel as if I am standing in the presence of a god. I shake my head slightly to bring myself back to reality. "See you later," I say, as we part ways toward our separate classes.

By lunchtime, I'm excited about my classes so far, hopeful that I will be challenged as well as staying interested in the subjects. I hurry to the cafeteria with my eyes open, looking for Em and Daniel. I spot Daniel first, but he is talking with his brother, so I beeline to the queue instead. Em walks up behind me in the line, touching my shoulder lightly to get my attention.

"I don't know if Daniel is going to join us," she says, gazing toward Daniel and Lucas.

I glance around the cafeteria. "Everyone is watching them. His brother must be really popular."

Em snorts. "He's football royalty. His oldest brother led the team to a state championship. Their father played, and his father before him. When Daniel took your hand earlier today, I thought I was going to faint dead away."

Suddenly, Daniel and Lucas turn in our direction, moving toward us with purpose. I grab Em's arm, squeezing tight, turning my focus with some effort to the guy in front of me in line, wearing his letterman's jacket even though it's August and hot as an oven. Em steps up beside me as if shielding me from the room. Surely, Lucas Bell doesn't plan on humiliating me further, this time in front of half the school?

I can feel my skin tingle, like Spidey sense, as Daniel and Lucas near. There's no one behind us in the line, so they fall into step right next to us. Daniel smiles warmly, tugging at his brother's sleeve. Lucas studies the cafeteria as if the last thing he wants to do is say something to me.

"Hi," Daniel says, his gaze bouncing back and forth between us. I notice how Lucas stands almost a head taller than his brother. Daniel orders, "Lucas has something t-to say."

When I get the courage to look up and up to his face, I find the Adonis from this morning surprisingly vanished. His eyes have lost that sharp edge, making him look more like an adorable puppy than a granite hero. He swallows, moving his Adam's Apple up and down. He really doesn't want to do this.

"I'm sorry about earlier," he blurts finally, shifting his broad shoulders. "I didn't mean anything by it, just that you're...," he lets the words trail off, leaving a bad taste to the air between us.

I cross my arms over my chest because I don't plan to give Lucas an inch. I turn to Daniel, ignoring his big brother. "At least Daniel is chivalrous," I say, softening the words because truly Daniel is the first boy to ever treat me nicely.

"He's always been the best one of us," Lucas says, raising his hand as if to scruff Daniel's hair, pulling it back just in time. The affection between brothers makes me forgive Lucas just a little bit.

Em nudges me as the line shifts forward. Thankful for the distraction, I move, pulling at the strap on my backpack. I feel a tap on my shoulder. Gritting my teeth, I turn, but luckily Lucas has disappeared, leaving only Daniel with his brown eyes shifting between Em and me.

"He really is s-sorry, D-dak-kota," he says.

"It's all right," I assure him. "I'm used to it."

"N-not anymore."

A heavy kind of silence descends after that. As the moments tick away, we get closer to the end of the long line. I'm starting to feel the pressure, wondering what to say next, when Em says into the void, "What is that?"

She purses her lips as we all turn to look at a large dish of greenish glop. "I hope they still have pizza," she says, and we all laugh, breaking the tension.

I'm not even hungry, but I know I have to eat something. Last year, the doctor diagnosed me with polycystic ovary syndrome, or PCOS. One of the things the disease does is make it hard for me to lose and maintain my weight. It also wreaks havoc on my emotions sometimes. So, yeah, high school is going to be some kind of challenge for me.

Picking out a small salad and an orange, I follow Em and Daniel to the table in the far reaches of the room where all the loners sit with their heads down, waiting for lunch to be over. Too bad we can't leave campus during lunch, like at my last school.

Now settled at the table, I fiddle with the food on my tray and study the other students through the veil of my eyelashes. I've never seen so many tall hairdos and boots. A heavy accent fills the air, drawing out the vowels, taking on a slow, wending pace that lulls me into a sense of safety. In fact, I'm just about to tell Em about how comfortable I am beginning to feel when the first glob of something slimy and wet smacks me in the side of the head and oozes its way down to my shoulder.

"Hey," Em and Daniel protest at once, each grabbing a napkin to help me wipe myself up.

"Don't protest," the skinny blond across the table from me advises. "You'll make it worse."

I feel Em draw into herself next to me, proof she knows the truth of that statement. Daniel scrapes his chair across the floor and stands up, glaring across the cafeteria. I think if he can figure out who threw the wad of greenish goop at me, he'll pummel them with the fists he's tapping against his thighs.

"Daniel."

I look up to see Lucas towering over us. He takes Daniel by the upper arm with one hand, grabs his brother's lunch tray with the other, and marches them both to the other side of the cafeteria. The way he does it, Daniel has no choice but to follow along. Every eye in the cafeteria follows their progression, watching them practically glide across the room.

And then the eyes turn back to me.

I want to shrink under the table and crawl out of the room. Instead, I force myself to take one bite of my salad, and then another, ignoring the pig noises in the background.

"I have science after lunch," Em says suddenly, her voice wooden. She lifts her pizza slice from her tray, watching it droop, her nose wrinkling. "I hope there aren't any weird smells," she adds, as if nothing has really happened.

"Thank you," I finally manage past the lump in my throat, "for sticking around."

Em's hand lays on top of mine, her finger's squeezing me. "We're the same, you and me," she explains. "I hope we can be friends forever."

Well, that does it. I feel the first tear slide down my cheek before I can stop it. "Friends forever," I agree.

The bell rings, bringing an end to the lunch period. Em and I part ways in the hall as I head to my English class, taking a quick break in the bathroom before to remove the last of the humiliating food stuck to me with a stench like rotten eggs. Walking into the classroom, I notice Daniel sitting in the back corner, his eyes on his spiral notebook as he sits flipping through the pages. I'm not going to sit through fifty minutes of American Lit wondering if Daniel ever plans to talk to me again, so I take a deep breath and walk right up to his desk.

"I'm sorry I embarrassed you," I blurt in greeting.

Daniel looks up, his face ashen. He tries to speak several times, his words coming out as just so many syllables, painfully slow. Finally, he rips a piece of paper from his spiral and writes, *My brother thinks he knows everything. He thinks I can't take care of myself. Can we forget about Lucas and lunch?*

I read the paper and look back up at him. "Sure," I agree, but my voice sounds wooden.

His shoulders pulls back as he picks nervously at the edge of his notebook. "W-want to go to the Dairy Queen a-after school?" he finally manages.

Despite his earlier kindness, his invitation now makes my defensive radar ping in my head. Boys who look like Daniel, related to high school royalty, don't want to be friends with a girl who looks like me. And he did abandon me at the first sign of trouble. If I agree to hang out with him, will I be hurting myself?

Daniel smiles sincerely, at least I tell myself so. Pushing down my concerns, I tell him I'd be glad to meet up after school before hurrying to an empty seat as the bell rings. I should ask Em to join us. After all, she's new to the school, too. My mother would have me ask her. Grace Fleming takes the meaning behind her name seriously, extending mercy every chance she gets.

"If it weren't for the merciful gift of salvation that Christ died on the cross to give all of us," she explains to people every chance she gets, "no one would be saved."

I see Em later during orchestra and decide to ask her to the Dairy Queen. Not going to lie. If Daniel plans to prank me, I'll appreciate having Em there as backup. As soon as the thought crosses my mind, I hear myself passing it along to her.

"It could be a set-up," I warn her. My mind flashes through images of other schools, plenty of places where someone went to that much trouble and more in order to poke fun at me.

She shrugs. "Still want to go?"

My backpack has made it through the first day. I hug it to my chest, thinking maybe that's some kind of sign. "Let's do it."

Turns out the Dairy Queen is a half block north of the football field. We walk there, trying not to sweat in the oppressive heat. As we pass the field, I see the team practicing. Lucas stands a head taller than the rest of his teammates. As

I'm watching, he seems to sense me, turning in our direction. A second later, he gets pummeled by one of his defense players. Somehow, it feels like a just consequence for his earlier behavior towards me.

"Where do you swim?" Em asks, bringing my attention back to her.

"We've rented a house with a pool. In Hawaii, I usually went to the Y or sometimes the ocean, but I was always afraid of being carried away by a riptide."

"You lived in Hawaii?"

"My dad's in the Army, so I've lived in a whole lot of places."

All kinds of cars fill the parking lot of the fast-food restaurant as we walk toward the small patio out front where a couple of bench tables are set up. Daniel sits at one, with two drinks on the table in front of him. I see a flicker of disappointment that shadows his smile for a brief second when he notices Em with me, but by the time we are at the table, he has stood to his full height, motioning for us to take a seat, his face beaming again.

"Hey, guys," he says, rubbing his hand on his neck. "Gee, I only g-got two s-sodas."

Em waves her hand. "Don't worry about it. I'm fine."

I push the soda in her direction. "You should drink it. My mom doesn't like me drinking sodas."

Crisis averted, we start discussing the first day of school. I think my orchestra leader, Mr. Mars, is going to be a super conductor. He has a picture of his schnauzer, Socks, on his desk and wears ties with pictures on them. Today's is filled with penguins. Em asks if Daniel will ever play football. He turns red explaining to us how far from football he hopes to be in high school.

"Look who we have here," a voice sing-songs, drawing the

attention of every student hanging out around us. "It looks like a minion."

I look down. I would choose today to wear my yellow dress. I turn to Em, purposefully ignoring my tormentor, to continue our private conversation. Of course, the taunting continues, as I hear others begin to snort like pigs.

Daniel slides to his feet, glaring at everyone, the muscle in the side of his neck pulsing. I reach out and grab his hand, pulling on it to get his attention. But my effort is useless because Em stands up next to Daniel, joining him in giving everyone hard looks.

"Shut up, Keenan," Daniel orders, "or I'll make you shut up." Surprisingly, he doesn't stutter.

The boy who called me a minion swallows and shifts his feet. "I didn't realize you liked them short and wide, Danny boy."

Before I can move, Daniel has taken Keenan by the collar and thrown him to the ground. Keenan lays there, winded. Taunted by the jeering of the crowd, he pushes himself back to his feet, giving an uppercut to Daniel's jaw. I watch my new friend's head snap back as Keenan throws his shoulder into Daniel. The next thing I know, I'm on the ground, my skirt swirling in the dirt around me. Unaware of my predicament, Daniel manages a jab to Keenan's stomach that causes the other boy to double over.

Regret forms a heavy ball inside my stomach as I fumble to get up and end this. Em's hand on my arm stops me just as the two boys grab each other and begin to wrestle. The noise of the crowd cheering the fight on reverberates in my head, coming to me as if down a long tunnel.

"I shouldn't have come here," I mouth to Em, who stands frozen not three feet away, her eyes wide as saucers. The hot sting of tears runs down my cheeks. She shakes her head, her lips moving jerkily, but I can't understand her words, especially since Keenan has just kicked Daniel's feet out from under him.

Suddenly, another ruckus seems to draw everyone's attention as half the football team, complete in workout gear, come jogging up to the restaurant. Leading the pack, Lucas looks as if he will kill Keenan as he reaches Daniel. The fight comes to an immediate end as Keenan stumbles back quickly, getting tangled in his own feet so that he lands with a thud on the concrete.

"What's going on here?" Lucas demands, his voice booming in the ominous silence.

Keenan swipes his bloody nose with the edge of his t-shirt. "All I did was say what everyone was thinking," he complains. "You called her a dwarf."

Lucas' hand flexes in and out of a fist. He glances at me, his eyes bouncing at and past me. "That was a mistake," he says, loud enough for everyone to hear.

Em and I hurry over to Daniel, pulling tissues out of our backpacks to blot at the blood dripping from a cut on his forehead. Lucas moves next to us, lifting Daniel's chin to view the damage. He turns back to the crowd. "From now on," he orders, "everyone will consider these three as being under my protection. Is that understood?"

When everyone just stands by silently watching the show, Lucas' teammates jostle each other. They give the students in the parking lot their fiercest glares. Then, in unison, as if it's a football drill, they grunt Lucas' question until the whole school answers yes.

"What are you looking at?" Lucas barks then. Suddenly, all the students decide they have somewhere else to be, dissipating like vapor from a cloud, leaving me, Em and poor Daniel standing in a semi-circle while half the football team look on.

Lucas turns to face us, studying Daniel's cuts and bruises. "Mom is going to kill me," he says.

Daniel laughs hollowly. "K-kill you? What about me?"

"You're her favorite," Lucas says.

"You can't get in trouble," I blurt. "It's all my fault."

Daniel reaches out, touching my face. His skin sealing to mine takes my breath away. "You're not to blame, Dakota," he says, glaring at the rest of the faces surrounding us.

Suddenly, Lucas reaches across to break the contact between me and his brother. "There shouldn't be anymore trouble," he says.

"D-don't you h-have p-p-p-practice?" Daniel asks. His words are slow, coming as if he has to squeeze them out.

Lucas' gives his brother a wry smile. "Yes, and if someone could stay out of trouble, I'd still be there."

He doesn't wait for a response, just turns and jogs away, followed by the rest of his team. We watch them disappear down the block and turn onto the field.

"Grams used to be a nurse," Em says, her voice crackling with tension. "We live just around the corner."

Daniel shakes his head. "I'll be okay."

I wince just looking at him. His left eye has almost swollen shut, and his upper lip oozes blood. "Are you sure?" I ask. "I feel so responsible."

He smiles. "Maybe you'll go to the movies with me on Friday, then."

Em and I have already planned to study at my house and watch TV that day, but now I feel as if I really owe Daniel. As if she can read my mind, Em gives me a nudge in Daniel's direction. "We can study on Saturday," she says, reading my mind.

And so begins perhaps the best three months of my life. Em and I become fast friends, the forever kind. I achieve first chair in the orchestra. Daniel takes me out for movies and picnics and even a day out on the lake in his father's fishing boat. He is kind and chivalrous, the best first boyfriend a girl could ask for. Thanks to Lucas' protection, no one makes fun of us, at least to our faces. The full meaning of a perfect life begins to take shape, fluttering its wings in my imagination, feeding my hope.

But all that changes on a frosty November evening when my parents ask me to join them in the living room for a family discussion. A cold shiver runs down my spine as I approach them because I know what a family talk means.

Mama's pretty face has that sad cast to it as I slip into the room and perch on the edge of the couch. Dad, usually comfortable in his easy chair, sits straight as a board, his hands clenched on his knees. My perfect life is over. I can see the shreds of it circling the soles of my orange Chucks and onto the brown shag rug.

My head snaps up from the floor, and I glare at my parents thinking *not this time.* "No," I say in the quiet of the room.

Dad sighs. "I'm sorry, pumpkin," he says.

"Dad won't have to be deployed anymore, Dakota. And there's a prep school that's willing to give you a full scholarship. Most of their students get into the Ivy League."

Something twists in my gut. I fiddle with the fabric of my skirt. "When?" I ask the rose petals on the cloth.

"You know the Army," Mama says.

I look at Dad. Even though his countenance is sad, his eyes are still as hard as steel. "Two weeks."

Sucking in a shaky breath, I resist the urge to wipe my face with my arm like a little kid. "Where?"

"Virginia," Dad answers.

"I really like it here," I whine.

Dad stands. "You're only a sophomore, kiddo. You'll bounce back from this."

It's an order, not a suggestion. He walks over, pats my shoulder awkwardly, and walks out, leaving a vacuum that sucks all the air out of the room. I know because suddenly I can't catch my breath.

My mother squats beside me, running her hand down my back and offering soothing whispers. Finally, my breathing comes back to normal. I want to rant and rave about the unfairness of it all, but instead I feel numb all over.

"You don't have to help me pack this time, sweetie," Mama says. "You can spend the two weeks with your friends."

But I'm a firm believer in ripping off the band-aid, a chip off Dad's block. I suck in a breath that hitches just below my diaphragm. "No, Mama. I'll help you. I'm glad Dad won't have to deploy anymore. He'll be safe this way."

My words sound wooden, rehearsed. Mama tuts, giving me a hug I don't want. "Think about your future, Dakota. You've wanted an Ivy League education since the sixth grade. Lincoln Prep may be just the avenue to get that for you. And you'll make new friends."

Mama is right. I do get the kind of education I'd always dreamed of. Friends? Well, thank goodness for Em in my life, despite the distance between us.

8 Years Later

I can't believe I'm running late. Again. Six months in Houston, and I still haven't gotten used to the traffic. I text Emily and settle back in the seat of my Uber, knowing this, at least, is out of my control.

Thankfully, I finally feel in control of everything else. After our move to Virginia, I fell apart for a while, even though I kept up my friendships with Em and Daniel with Zoom sessions. My parents even paid for me to go visit that summer. That's when I met Delaney, a tall, svelte beautiful blond who thought Daniel hung the moon. I couldn't even work up the heat to blame her for stealing Daniel from me. He was the best of boyfriends, and Delaney was there.

I returned to Virginia downtrodden but determined. Soon enough, the challenges of a Lincoln Prep education consumed me, especially the desire to do my best academically, as well as having the kind of rounded resume that would impress a school like Harvard. Mama found a naturopathic doctor for me. With changes to my diet and a few supplements, I started to see changes in my body. I also had a growth spurt, adding a couple of inches to my frame.

Today, I'm closer to 135 pounds than 180. After my five years at Harvard obtaining an MBA, I found a job in Houston working for a company that deals with oil futures. I'm the low girl on the totem pole today, but I have an ambitious five-year plan, and I aim to achieve it.

Em finished high school, even though her grandmother died her senior year. She decided to be called Emily then because she was by herself, and Emily sounded more like the name of a woman who could brave the wide world all on her own. After graduation, she worked two jobs to put herself through community college. Now, she works as a vet tech at a clinic that deals with large animals as well as domestic pets. We've been roommates since I took the job in Houston.

We're meeting up tonight at a fancy steak restaurant in the Galleria area to celebrate Emily's 23rd birthday. If I have transformed from my dwarf past, Emily has metamorphosized like a butterfly bursting from its cocoon. Her freckles, once so prominent, have faded to a sprinkling that highlight her high cheekbones and emerald eyes. She now stands 5'11", with a body built like a model.

I finally reach the restaurant. Entering through its thick, glass doors, I immediately see Emily sitting at a corner booth with her fiancé, Neill, right beside her. He's on a commercial construction crew, six feet tall and solid like a brick wall. His beefy arm is draped across the bench behind Emily's shoulders, protectively. I feel a stab of jealousy slice through my chest, just a brief pain that I push back down again, ashamed of myself.

I should get up the courage to ask Leon in accounting out for a coffee. He's only a few inches taller than I am, with thick, wavy hair and kind eyes. I'm pretty sure he likes cats, too, which is good because I have two of them living in the apartment I share with Emily.

Pushing these thoughts aside, I sing out, "Happy Birthday," as I slide into the booth opposite my best friend. "You look fantastic," I say, extending the present I have for her across the table in my open palm.

Emily eyes the long, thin box suspiciously. "You know I don't want expensive things," she protests.

"Open it," I urge, trying and failing to hide a smile.

She fumbles with the silver ribbon and red wrapping paper, finally freeing the lid and opening the box to reveal the vintage *Hello Kitty* necklace I'd found for her in a thrift shop almost three months before. I don't know how I hung on to it for so long.

"It's perfect," she exclaims, giving me her most brilliant smile. She turns and lifts her hair so that Neill can help her put the Chatzky on.

"When I saw it, I knew it had your name written all over it," I say. "How are the wedding plans going?"

Emily looks over at Neill with a secret kind of smile that warms me and makes me feel my loneliness at the same time. "We have so much to tell you; let's order dinner first."

We've ordered our steaks and sides and are sipping on iced tea and nibbling on bread as Emily begins to detail their recent cake-tasting outing, the decorations she plans for us to make for the church and our trip this coming weekend to the bridal shop to look for a wedding dress. Suddenly, Emily pales like she's seen a ghost, reaching across to grab my hand and squeezing it in a death grip.

"Don't turn around," she says, so of course, I want to turn around. It takes everything in me to keep my eyes trained on hers, which have gone round with wonder.

"What is it, babe?" Neill asks, tightening his grip on her.

She opens her mouth to answer, but she's interrupted by a deep, slightly familiar male voice. "Is that really you, Emily?" it says.

I look up and gasp. Standing at our table is Lucas Bell, tall and every bit as handsome as he was in high school. A thin, tall brunette, pretty with flawless skin like porcelain, clings to his arm, holding her left hand in such a way as to show off the five-carat engagement ring on her finger.

My gasp finally registers with Lucas, who turns to see me sitting there. All the blood seems to drain from his face. "Dakota Fleming?" he asks.

I laugh at the sound of his incredulity, which has broken the spell of seeing him again so unexpectedly. "Have I really changed so much?" I tease.

He ignores that. "What are you doing here?"

"Oh, Lucas," the woman says, her voice gentle, but firm, "this is starting to sound like an interrogation."

He pats her hand. "I'm sorry, Amelia. This is Emily and Dakota. They were Daniel's friends back in high school."

"Did I hear my name?" another voice asks from behind me.

Emily's eyes are like saucers. I turn to see a grown-up version of Daniel, a good five inches taller than the last time I saw him, with a rugged jawline, wearing a tailored suit and looking like a million bucks.

If Lucas' suit is expensive, Daniel's could cost a year's wage. I guess that's what you can afford when you play professional ball. Ironically, Daniel rather than Lucas turned out to have the talent that rocketed him past mere high school football to NFL fame. He had a career-ending injury last year, but I can't tell it as he stands here looking perfectly god-like.

"It's Emily and Dakota," Lucas says unnecessarily, "you know, from high school."

Daniel doesn't answer right away. I can't blame him. Sitting here, not three feet from him after all these years, I feel sixteen again. My heart skitters sideways in my chest as I try to look cool, even though I can feel the heat building in my cheeks.

He studies me for a moment that stretches. "It's good to see you both again," he finally says, his stutter completely absent, along with the softer lines of youth in his face and silhouette.

"We should meet up some time, to catch up, I mean," Lucas says, giving his fiancé Amelia a wary glance.

She forces a tense grin to her lips. "I think that invitation should be up to Daniel, sweetheart," she clips out. "After all, they're his old friends."

The way she emphasizes the word *old* reminds me of that

first day of sophomore year when Lucas called me a dwarf in front of my entire homeroom, likewise dismissing me. Maybe Daniel also sees me as someone to dismiss. I hold my breath as he reaches inside his suit jacket and retrieves a business card, laying it on the table between us and staring at it a moment before finally meeting my eyes.

My head buzzes with a noise like a loud, ringing bell, and my stomach fills with fluttering butterflies. Suddenly, my lips are so dry.

"I think that sounds like a great idea," he says. He stuffs his hands deep in his pockets as if to keep them to himself. "Give me a call."

"We'd better let these people get back to their dinner now," Amelia purrs, tugging lightly on Lucas' arm.

I watch them walk away, my fingers covering the business card and pinning it to the table as I concentrate on breathing normally so I don't hyperventilate.

"You never told me you knew *the* Daniel Bell," Neill accuses us as we all turn back to stare at the bread bowl in the center of our table.

Emily shrugs, tears off a piece of bread and throws it at him playfully. "It was a long time ago," she says. "Do you think they looked the same?"

This last is addressed at me. I can't concentrate. The feelings I had for Daniel back in high school have just exploded like a nuclear bomb in my chest. I place my hand on my sternum and rub.

"Are you okay?" Emily asks.

I take a drink of water, and my throat feels tight. "Is it warm in here?" I laugh at myself. "I'll be fine. I think I'm going to run to the bathroom before the food arrives, though."

"Want me to go with you?" Emily gives me a look that says I'm fooling no one.

I shake my head in answer and rise to unsteady feet. The bathroom is on the other end of the restaurant, luckily in the opposite direction of the Bell brothers. Down a long hallway, I twist and wind until I reach the little alcove with the doorway to the ladies' room. Once inside, I move to the sink, turning on the cold water and splashing my face with it until my mascara runs down my cheeks.

Patting my face dry with one of the thick, soft paper towels the restaurant provides, I use my fingers to un-smudge my makeup, then take a few deep breaths. Looking in the mirror, I tell myself to woman up as an image of Daddy's disapproving face flashes in front of me. I'm a Harvard graduate and a Fleming. Impossible crushes will not get the best of me.

I open the restroom door, ready to give my brave face to the world, when I run straight into a wall of muscle. I fall back against the closed door, my hands plastered against the cool wood. "I'm sorry," I tell the fourth button on his expensive shirt.

Instead of stepping back to give me space, Daniel stays where he is, the scent of his cologne filling my nostrils. "You've changed," he says, not hiding his surprise.

I manage to shrug like I don't have a care in the world, even though my heart feels like it is beating out of my chest. Maybe that's why all I manage are choppy, short sentences. "Eight years is a long time. You look like you're doing well. I'm sorry about your shoulder."

I glance up just in time to see his jaw tick. "It only hurts on days that end in *y*," he says, reaching out to finger one of my curls. "I miss you and high school," he breathes out. I'm not sure he meant for me to hear the words.

"I don't like to think about high school anymore. It seems like a lifetime ago, and I hope I'm a completely different person than I was back then." I swallow, thinking about Delaney suddenly, the girl Daniel chose when I moved to Virginia. "I mean, who stays the same?"

He doesn't answer, just keeps looking at me like I'm a specimen in a jar. As I watch, he leans in, placing his lips on mine. They feel warm, comforting. I hope he doesn't notice I have no idea what to do with my lips as he continues to press his mouth to mine. I breathe him in, and time seems to slow down.

Too soon, he pulls back, and a sly grin distorts his features. "I've been wanting to do that since the last time you came to Texas."

The mention of that visit, when he'd moved on to someone new, curdles something in my stomach. My smile turns into a frown as I flatten my hands against Daniel's chest and push, giving me room to step out of his loose embrace, giving me space.

"You mean when you were dating someone else," I say as my fingers curl into fists by my side.

"Excuse me," a soft voice insists from over my shoulder. I turn to see an older woman in a fancy suit, clutching the pearls around her neck with twitchy fingers.

"Sorry to block your way," I mumble, moving closer to the wall so that she can pass. This gives me the perfect excuse to hurry back down the hall, but my feet refuse to move.

The woman takes a step forward, then stops to look at us. "You remind me of my Edward and me. What a cute couple. Don't let silly arguments get between you."

She turns then, walking into the bathroom and leaving us alone. I glance at Daniel, but my gaze skitters past him to the wall behind. "It was nice to see you again," I say, finally making my feet work. Any moment now, Emily will come looking for me, find me cornered here with Daniel, and then how embarrassed will I be?

"Wait," Daniel says as he grabs my arm lightly, stopping my forward motion. I keep my eyes turned away from him. "At least give me your number," he adds.

"Why?"

I do turn then to see Daniel giving me an incredulous look. "Because I'd like to get to know you again, Dakota Fleming."

My brain skitters to a halt. The next thought isn't a pleasant one: *Wasn't it fortunate he ran into me at this lovely restaurant, to remind him I was someone in this world*, I ask myself. Shaking my head to push away any other sarcastic thoughts, I reach out my hand to take his phone. The fingers putting my information into his cell shake slightly. Silly me. I hand his phone back to him. "Now, I really have to get back to Emily and Neill before they send out a search squad," I say, turning and practically running down the hall and back into the main restaurant before Daniel can say anything more.

The steaks have arrived by the time I scooch back into the booth, feeling all kinds of flustered. Neill opens his mouth, but Emily, always my protector, elbows him in the ribs to stop him from asking any questions. I dig into my steak, which smells like heaven and tastes like sawdust in my mouth.

Somehow, I manage to finish the meal, returning almost completely to myself by the time the waiter brings us the small, but beautifully decorated cake Neill has had the restaurant prepare especially for Emily's birthday.

As she blows out the candles, closing her eyes to make her wish, my cell pings:

Unknown: You look like an angel in that candlelight.

. . .

Unknown: This is Daniel, BTW.

I turn my phone off to give Emily my whole attention. She reaches across the table and grabs my hand. "Thank you for coming. It wouldn't have been a proper birthday without you."

I can't say anything because my throat has tightened up. Looking across at Emily and Neill, I realize a time will come when I won't be welcome to something. Emily's bond to me will have to shift when she becomes Neill's wife.

Moments later, we are waiting for our car by the valet stand, Neill and Emily holding hands and me feeling more like a third wheel than usual. As if she can sense my melancholy, Emily nudges me with her shoulder, leaning down to whisper into my ear.

"You okay?"

I nod, forcing a smile to my lips. "Yes, of course."

"Then, why did you turn off your phone?"

Neill tugs at Emily's hand. "This is us."

Saved by the F-150. I climb into the extended cab, leaning the side of my head against the cool glass. I'm clutching my phone in one hand, arguing with myself about turning it back on. I need to face the truth: Daniel Bell, who could have any woman in the universe, can't be interested in me.

By the time Neill pulls into a space in our apartment complex, I want nothing more than to take a hot shower and curl up in bed. I leave the lovebirds outside near the truck to say good-bye and make my way up to our apartment. I'm in the shower with my eyes closed, allowing myself to think about Daniel kissing me, when I feel a cold shaft of air. My eyes fly open.

Emily stands waving my phone in front of her body. "Daniel has sent you ten messages. I think he still likes you, Dakota. I doubt he ever stopped liking you. Call him."

I stop the shower, grabbing a towel from the rack and wrapping it around my body with jerky movements. "My phone was off, Em."

Her face drops. "I just got excited for you."

"Don't. Emily, I'm not going to start dating Daniel Bell, who could have anyone, by the way."

Emily bites her lip. "He didn't seem to want anyone but

you when he cornered you in the hallway."

"You saw that?" I exclaim.

Emily grins. "I got worried about you."

"Well, there's nothing to worry about because that's the last time I'll see Daniel, superstar, Bell."

"I don't see what his stardom has to do with it," Emily says, cocking her head, studying me. "Don't be afraid."

The accusation makes me think of my father standing over me on so many occasions and saying the same thing. I feel my back stiffen. "I'm going to bed."

"Don't be like that," she says, following me.

"Like what?" I pull on my nightshirt, letting the comfy material cascade over me, down past my knees. I root in my underwear drawer for my most comfortable panties and slip them on next.

Emily watches me from the bedroom doorway. "You're better than the Daniel Bells of this world deserve."

The words come out of her mouth sincerely enough, but they enter my ears sounding like my mother's voice, encouraging me when we both knew I had no chance. I flash back to that time shortly after we'd moved to Virginia when Daddy insisted I join the long-distance track team. He woke me up at 4 am every morning for months and ran with me for miles before going to work for the day. Mama helped by going with me to the gym during the afternoons, overseeing my strength training. When I still failed to run fast enough for the team, Daddy shook his head with a tense set to his lips. Mama, she put her arm around my shoulders and reminded me how well I'd done on my grades.

I throw myself on the bed and pull my pillow against my chest. Emily finally enters the room, jumping onto the bed beside me. "Are you going to answer him back?" she asks, handing me my phone.

Closing my eyes, I throw my head back. "No, I think I am going to finally get up the courage to ask out Leon from work."

Emily groans. "He's so ordinary."

"Just what I need," I agree.

"You'll get bored."

"Better bored than devastated."

Emily takes my hand, twining our fingers. We both look at the neatly-trimmed nails on our twin manicures. We went to the salon earlier in the week as part of her birthday. "Neill had to ask me out a half dozen times before I finally accepted. I've never told you before, but he doesn't just work the construction crew, Dakota. His family owns a huge housing development firm, and they do industrial construction, too. I don't belong in their world at all, but I love him so much, I'm willing to take the chance."

I have to push my jaw up with my free hand to close my mouth. "Why didn't you tell me?"

"I don't know. At first, I figured he'd dump me after a few dates anyway. Then, I guess I was afraid to talk about it. I didn't want to jinx it, you know?"

"But you're sure now," I say more than ask.

She nods, and her face gets that dreamy look to it that always happens when she thinks about Neill. "I am so sure." She picks at the pink coverlet on top of my bed. "You'll think about giving Daniel a chance, won't you? You two were so cute back in high school."

I set my phone on top of my nightstand. "I doubt he asks me out. He probably sent all these texts sitting in the restaurant because he was bored or something."

She shakes her head, and then a huge yawn overtakes her. "I'm going to bed. Work starts early in the morning."

I watch her leave the bedroom before wiggling myself

under the covers. I pray sleep overcomes my racing mind, even as an image of Daniel fills my brain.

He can't be as wonderful and strong and kind a person on the inside as he looks like on the outside, that wonderful adult I thought he'd grow to be when we dated in high school. That's the last thought I have before falling into a deep sleep.

∞ ∞ ∞

Work seems more hectic than usual, maybe because I spend most of the morning trying to figure out how I can "accidentally" run into Leon around lunch time and ask him to join me for a sandwich at the little shop on the lobby floor of our high-rise office building.

Around 11:30, I return to my office after a trip to the copy room only to find an overly-large bouquet of flowers sitting in the middle of my desk. I glance behind me to see what looks like the entire floor of personnel staring at me, snickering. Getting flustered, I push my office door shut and close the blinds that stand between me and everyone else before studying the bouquet more closely to find the card that came with it.

For all the flowers I never got to give you. –Daniel

My legs won't hold me up anymore. I slide down the side of my desk and land on the floor with a little oomph that seems forced out of my body. After a few, deep breaths, I reach over and behind me to grope blindly on my desk for my cell phone.

Emily picks up on the first ring. "What's up?"

"You got a minute?" I ask.

"Hold on," she says, and the line mutes for one minute, then two. "Okay, I'm all yours. What's going on?"

"The biggest bouquet I've seen in my life is sitting in the middle of my desk. I had to close all the blinds to my office just to ward off the stares," I tell her in a hushed voice.

"Told you Daniel was interested. You should call and thank him for them."

"I can't," I say, shaking my head as if she can see me. "What would I have to say?"

Emily pauses. "Um, thank you," she finally says.

"Beyond that. He's famous, and I'm me. I don't see this going anywhere."

"You're just afraid to give him a chance."

I stand and begin pacing in front of my desk. "We had our chance, back in high school. People like me, we don't get second chances. And besides, I think I should move forward with my idea about Leon in accounting."

"With all the flowers Daniel just sent you? Text me some pictures, will you? It's rude not to at least call and say thank you. Ten seconds, fifteen tops, and you'll be in and out of the conversation."

"I just don't want," I stop the excuse that is about to come tumbling out of my mouth. I bite my lower lip so hard, I wince. "I'm afraid, Em," I admit.

"Oh, Dakota, it wouldn't mean anything if you weren't just a little afraid. I'd probably be terrified, too." I hear a rustle of movement in the background, then Emily returns. "I have to go. Dakota, don't be a scaredy cat. Look what being a lion got me."

The call clicks to an abrupt end, and I stand with my dead phone plastered to my ear, wondering at my sudden timidity. So much for thinking I'd come a long way since high school. What am I going to do?

As if in answer to my question, there's a timid knock at my door, and Leon from accounting stands on the other side when I open it. He's holding a few folders in his hand.

"I need to go over," he begins, but stops as soon as he sees the huge bouquet on my desk. "Oh my, did you get engaged or something?"

I shake my head. "These are just from an old friend."

"It looks like a lifetime's worth of flowers." Leon squints at the array of roses, gardenias and calla lilies as if he is assessing a tallied receipt. "You have some rich friends."

"They are a lifetime's worth of flowers," I say, squaring my shoulders because Leon's comments are beginning to sound like an insult to my already sensitive ears. I glance at the bouquet again, and I'm struck with a profound sense of sadness. In a way, those flowers represent all the love I've missed trying to make the best grades, go to an Ivy League college and succeed with my career.

Turning back to Leon, I have every intention of asking him to join me for lunch, even if he's currently backing away from me as if I'm one of those high maintenance girls a man who tracks dollars for a living can't handle. I open my mouth, only to have my jaw drop further.

"Are you all right?" Leon asks. "You look like you've seen a ghost."

"Just me," Daniel says, standing behind Leon. His presence sucks all the air out of the room. He's wearing a University of Houston t-shirt, jeans and Ropers. As I stand there like a statue, he adjusts the baseball cap on his dark hair and tugs at the strap on his backpack. "Am I interrupting?"

Leon turns, and now it's his turn for a jaw to drop. "Aren't you Daniel Bell?" He glances back at the flowers. "That explains the bouquet."

"Could you give us a moment, Leon?" I ask, finding my voice, which comes out sharply, making me cringe.

Daniel steps inside, closing the door on Leon and the rest of the office. He lays his backpack on my guest chair and stuffs his hands in his pockets like he doesn't know where to put them.

The gesture seems so transparent, so *human*, that I forget his superstar football status.

We stand staring at each other for a few, long breaths. I'm trying to remember if I put on my favorite dress today, the one that makes me look especially skinny and tall, without peeking down the length of me. At the same time, I want a pair of sunglasses to reduce the glare of Daniel's brilliant smile. In this casual wear, he seems more handsome than he did at the restaurant, all dressed up in his three-piece Armani. How is that possible?

"I just finished classes and thought I'd drop by. I was hoping you'd like to do lunch together."

"Classes?" I say stupidly, totally ignoring his invitation.

"I'm enrolled at U of H, in the school of architecture. What with the pros recruiting me my junior year and this and that, I never finished my program."

"There are plenty of beautiful women on campus," I hear myself say, now sounding like a jealous loser. I move around to behind my desk, putting my palms on the glass protective cover to steady myself.

My stomach drops when I look up and realize I am now completely hidden behind the bouquet. The only way Daniel can see me is over the arc of colorful petals, giving the man a perfect view of the top of my head. I wonder if my part is straight.

"So, are you free for lunch?" he asks again, gracefully ignoring my silliness. I can hear the cockiness of his smile in the tone of his question, even if I can't see his face.

I grab my purse and come around the desk again. "I have an hour," I blurt, my fingers moving nervously on the strap. "Where would you like to go?"

He shoulders his backpack, takes my hand and places it in the crook of his arm. His muscles are hard, and his skin feels smooth and warm. "Wherever you are, darling," he says, sending shivers down my spine.

I press my fingers into his flesh. "That sounds like the kind of line you've used many a time before," my smart mouth blurts before I can stop it. Oh, well, he might as well know from the outset that my lips tend to go before my brain can catch up to them.

"I don't use cheesy lines," he replies, unaffected. "Every line I use is completely sincere."

We reach the bank of elevators. A few of the people in our lobby area start staring and pointing at us. Daniel reaches up to pull his cap further down, over his eyes. He breaks the contact of my hand so he can put his arm over my shoulder and pull me closer, as if I too must disappear.

When we stand alone in the elevator finally, the doors closed, he takes his arm away from me, giving us distance. He adjusts the backpack strap again, like a nervous habit.

"Sorry about that," he apologizes softly.

I try to look him in the eye, but his ballcap still covers his face. "I'm sure that happens to you all the time."

"Not as often as it used to. At least there's one good thing about not playing football anymore."

His voice sounds wistful. I don't think he realizes it. "Since we're being honest," I say, "why don't you admit that you haven't thought about me one time since that summer of our junior year?"

He looks down at his Ropers, answering my question with one of his own, "You don't have a fella, do you?"

The doors to the elevator open. He takes my hand, entwining our fingers this time. I look down at them, mine almost childlike encased in his like this. "I've never gotten around to it, having a boyfriend, that is."

He looks down at me, giving me a full-on view of his manly perfection. "Lucky me, then."

We walk down the street to a corner café. The baseball cap screws down on his head again. I think how sad to live hiding in plain sight. Then I realize maybe I've done the same, avoiding serious relationships because they might get in the way of my quest to prove myself to Daddy and to turn myself into Mama, no matter how impossible either feat.

"You dumped me," I blurt once the waitress has come and gone from our table.

His shoulders slump. "That was a lifetime ago, Dakota Fleming. Can't you just forget about it? Haven't I asked you to forgive me?"

"It's not about forgiving," I insist, swallowing the lump in my throat. "It has been a lifetime, and yours has been very different from mine."

"But we don't have to have lived the same lives for me to know that you are still as smart and kind behind that beautiful façade as you ever were."

"I could have changed," I mumble. Hope, long since dormant, flutters anemically in my chest.

"Only for the better," Daniel insists, picking up his glass as if to give me a toast. "To Dakota, the girl of my dreams," he says.

I sit there looking at my glass of water instead of lifting it, feeling that hope strengthen in my chest. After a moment, Daniel clears his throat.

"You'll never know if you don't give it a try," he coaxes.

That's when I decide dreams may rarely come true but they can never come true if we don't give them a chance.

Or a second chance, as the case may be.

----*The End*-----

Freefall

A Novella

> *"I have said these things to you, that in me you may*
> *have peace. In the world you will have tribulation.*
> *But take heart; I have overcome the world."*
> JOHN 16:33 (ESV)

Dee Culperson and Tank Brand could not come from more varied backgrounds. She's a kindergarten teacher , petite in size but bold and bubbly (on the outside, at least). Tank, just retired from the special forces, stands six-foot-four in his stocking feet, his life confrontation and struggle.

When circumstances bring them together, will they both notice the invisible, common thread that pulls them together? Tank knows what it means to lose, which may be what draws him to Dee, who carries secrets that have closed her off from the one, true relationship that matters, her commitment to her Savior God.

Can these two, wounded souls help each other understand God's love for them? Will finding each other help them discover the true nature of God when it comes to tragedy? That only through Jesus may the world be overcome?

Chapter One

Tucker "Tank" Brand scanned the crowded bar, his practiced gaze taking in the rowdy group of college frat boys jostling around the pool tables in the corner, the biker hunching over the bar at six o'clock, his body language giving off an aura that kept a neat, three-foot perimeter around him, the lone man in the corner making sinister eyes at some of the women dancing under the strobe lights. He shook his head and forced his shoulders to relax, reminding himself he was just any other civilian now, not the Special Forces Captain he'd been for the last seven years of his twenty-year career.

That was gone now, replaced by an empty space he had yet to fill. He shook the thought away and stepped farther into the bar, as the people in front of him parted like the Red Sea, noting his six-foot-four, muscular frame out of the corner of their wide eyes. The bolder ones, all women, met his narrow, brown-eyed glare with sparkling invitation in their gazes, looks he ignored as he strode to the bar, easily catching the bartender's attention and ordering a beer on tap.

His second beer sat half full when the commotion started, a crashing of glass followed by a shriek that echoed in the sudden silence. Tank's head shot instinctively to the noise, his eyes taking in the medium-height cowboy with his Stetson sitting askew on his blonde head, a blush visibly creeping up his long neck. He dismissed the cowboy in a millisecond, as the woman standing in front of the other man, her fists cocked on her hips, took all Tucker's attention.

She was small, probably a good foot shorter than Tucker, with blonde hair that shone in the strobe lights and hung like a curtain down her back. She had a slight build, too, with curves in just the right places to look like a woman. If it weren't for those breasts, Tucker thought dispassionately, others might just mistake her for a kid.

She turned on her heel then, giving Tank a clearer view of her face with its full, thick lips and long lashes over eyes green like emeralds. Her beauty took his breath away. He shifted on the bar stool and watched as she moved toward him, tucking her hair behind her left ear, muttering to herself, two bright, pink orbs forming on her high cheekbones.

Tank stood up and inched his way toward her, forming a blocking wall as she hurried past. She barreled into him, clutching at his belt to prevent a fall.

"This was a mistake," she blurted to the buttons on his polo shirt. Then, her hands still gripping his belt, she trailed her eyes up and up, following the line of his polo past his thick, muscled neck until she met his brown eyes. "Oh," she exclaimed, stepping back again, her fingers still tucked lightly into his pants, "you're so talllll."

She drew out this last, her lips forming an adorable sort of pout that made Tank's fingers twitch. He hitched up one eyebrow and grinned. He opened his mouth, readying a witty reply, when another voice interrupted him.

"Well, I like this, Dee," a nasally twang drawled. "Accusing me of being forward, and you've got your hands down another man's pants."

The blush blooming up her neck and across her cheeks now, *Dee* stared at her hands, a horrified expression flashing across her emerald eyes. She yanked herself away from Tank so quickly that she lost her balance and would have gone flying across the floor had he not snaked out one large hand and steadied her by the upper arm.

Her free hand flew up to her chest, where she fisted the muslin material of her summer dress and opened and closed her mouth like a guppy before managing. "I'm so sorry, sir. I'm so embarrassed, I could just sink right through the floor."

She had a southern lilt to her voice, not quite Texan, not Georgia peach, either. Tank lightened his grip on her forearm and stroked the bare skin beneath her cap sleeve. "Most people call me Tank, darlin'," he told her, winking. "You say sir and I'm looking around for my grandfather."

"Don't waste your breath, Mister," the cowboy continued as if Tank had been talking to him. "This one's frigid."

Dee whirled on her heel, effectively pulling herself out of Tank's loose grasp. She pointed her finger, her nail trimmed close and buffed to a shine, into the cowboy's chest, emphasizing each of her words. "I told you I was a nice girl," she declared, her body vibrating with her conviction, forcing the cowboy to take several steps back. "I told you getting frisky wasn't going to get you anywhere."

A cat call sounded from the far corner of the room, and Tank realized with a start that the vivacious Dee had so diverted him that he hadn't felt the entire bar taking in the show. He settled back on his bar stool, away from the attention, and took another long drag on his beer. Dee, meanwhile, pulled her hand back to her side and rolled back her shoulders. With her head held high, she made her way through the crowd, which parted in amusement as she passed, and strode out the front door.

Tank threw a twenty onto the bar and followed the tiny powerhouse as the crowd closed back in on itself. He stepped outside and inhaled the sweet scent of hay on the air, a refreshing change from the cigarette smoke and alcohol that clung to his clothes and thick hair. He spotted her under the street lamp about twenty yards down the road, a cellphone in her hand, her wide eyes darting back and forth as if she thought she might be set upon any minute.

He approached on not-so-stealthy feet to avoid startling her, his hands hanging loose at his sides, his face as neutral as he could make it. She inched up against the lamp post when she noticed him, holding the cell phone between them as if it were a weapon.

"Hello again," she blurted. "Thank goodness for Uber, right?"

It was on his lips to offer her a ride, but she seemed to sense his intent, drawing even further into herself. Tank set back on his heels, a cold feeling dampening his interest. Maybe she was just a kid after all. "I'll watch out for you until your Uber gets here," he offered instead. "I won't let anyone hurt you."

Her blush returned, and she bit her lower lip as if contemplating whether she could take him at his word. Tank wondered if she was a good girl or just a very good actress. She seemed to make up her mind, taking a small step in his direction and giving a tiny nod of her head.

"Thank you," she said, then chuckled at herself. "This whole night has been a disaster. I'm sure I don't have to tell you I don't usually frequent bars."

Tank crossed his arms in front of his chest, starting to feel just a little put upon if he were being honest with himself. "Are you even legal, darlin'?"

She flipped her head, causing her hair to shroud her upper body. "I'm legal, Tank," she answered, emphasizing his name so that her lips seemed to bite down on the word, "just not very wise, apparently."

They stood in silence then, the jangly sound of the music from the bar floating on the air around them, voices fading in and out as the doors opened and closed over the next several minutes. Finally, he took a step closer to her, ramming his hands into his pockets.

"What do you do when you're not standing outside bars waiting for an Uber?" Tank asked her.

Dee shook her head. "I'm a football coach, can't you tell?"

Tank snorted. "Bet you don't even need a whistle."

She shrugged and deadpanned. "I just grab them by the pants."

Before Tank could react, she shifted on her feet. "These heels are killing me." Looking at him through the veil of her long hair, she asked, "Mind if I take them off?"

Tank felt a muscle in his jaw twitch. What was it about this little slip of a thing? "Really, what do you do?" he asked, watching with interest as she slipped out of the heels without waiting for his answer, dangling them from her fingers.

Her head was laying back on her neck as she stretched and scrunched her freed toes. He noticed the nails, once hidden by her pumps, now visible and painted a ruby red. A hint of her perfume, subtle but pretty, wafted into his nose. Just when he thought she hadn't heard or would refuse to answer the question, she looked at him again with a satisfied smile on her face. "I teach kindergarten," she told him, "not much call for fancy heels." She waved the pumps in front of her and sighed.

"I'm surprised you get away with that hair in a classroom," he motioned toward the silky strands falling below her waist.

She smiled. "It's usually braided and wound around my head. My daddy used to call this style, hanging long and loose, my naughty hair."

Tank edged another step closer, feeling pulled as if by an invisible magnet. "So, what would Daddy say about your naughty hair tonight?" he teased her.

"He's a minister, actually, Southern Baptist, back home where our congregation has about three hundred members, all of whom would be mortified if they knew the mess I got myself into tonight, especially Daddy."

Tank felt his collar grow too tight. He'd known his share of preacher's daughters through the years, but none of them quite like Dee. He frowned. "So, you weren't kidding when you said that about being good back there, huh? You're not one of those preacher's kids who get up to no good?"

Her cheeks turned red once more. "Well, I'm not perfect, not by a long shot, but I'm not loose, either." She sat her shoes on the ground and shoved her phone into one of them, then took a step in Tank's direction, crowding his space. "This is a personal kind of conversation to be having with a complete stranger," she said, foisting out her hand. "My name's DeAnna Harriett Culperson, but my friends call me Dee. Who are you when you're at home, Tank?"

Instead of answering her question, he cocked his head and chuckled. "Your students must think you're hilarious," he said.

She grinned. "My Daddy says I'm forthright is all."

Her hand was still suspended between them. Tank clasped it with one hand, noting how dainty it felt, and pulled her gently into his body. She stiffened but didn't pull away. Surprisingly, she laughed and stepped on top of Tank's perfectly-polished Ropers, throwing back her head so she could still see his eyes.

"I think it might take three of me to make one of you," she teased, bouncing slightly on his feet.

He leaned down until his lips were just inches from her own. "More like six," he breathed out, taking in the scent of peppermint mouthwash on her breath and the sparkle in her emerald eyes this close, as if he might drown in them.

She slipped out of his grasp and stepped away from him then, chuckling nervously and shoving her hair back behind her ear. Tank felt grateful for the separation. It gave him the opportunity to cool his jets. If she were truly a nice girl as she claimed, she had no business getting mixed up with the likes of Tank Brand.

An older model Ford pulled up to the curb. "That's my ride," she said.

Tank felt a pang in his gut, the same kind of eerie feeling that had saved him through the years in many a combat situation. He glanced around the perimeter quickly, searching for signs of danger. When none appeared, he had to admit that the pang came from a different root cause. He watched Dee crouch down to retrieve her shoes and phone, then turn around to face him, an apologetic look on her pretty face.

"I'm sorry I was so much trouble, Tank." She put out her hand, and he shook it briefly, letting their hands part as if watching the scene play out in slow motion in front of him.

She turned to go. She would get inside the Ford, the engine

of which her driver impatiently gunned, and speed out of his life forever if he didn't do something. "Where do you teach?" he heard himself blurting out just as Dee's dainty hand grabbed hold of the door handle.

She looked up, startled. "Kennedy Elementary," she told him. "Why?"

He shrugged. "I just wanted to know who the lucky students were, that's all."

"Ahh, you're a sweetheart," she sighed, before giving him a slight wave and hopping into the car.

Tank walked back into the bar shaking his head. In all his 38 years, he'd been called any number of things, but never before had anyone called the giant of a man a sweetheart.

Chapter Two

Dee sat in the back seat of the Ford, clasping and unclasping her hands. What a silly, silly mess she'd made of trying something new and adventurous. She glanced down at the form-fitting dress and high-heeled shoes so different from her usual outfits and felt her skin crawl.

If the tall man who'd taken pity on her knew how she usually dressed, in her button-down dress shirts and pencil skirts that fell well past her knees, he'd probably turn running in the other direction. Of course, he didn't look like the kind of man who would run from anything.

She blushed, thankful for the darkness that surrounded her, just thinking about how brazen she'd been to stand right up on top of the poor man's boots like that. She'd seen something in his deep, brown eyes then, something more than the interest a man might have in a woman. A sadness, the kind that cut bone deep, seemed to peer at her from behind those long, thick lashes.

Dee knew what that kind of sorrow felt like, how it weighed down on a person even on good days when the sun shone bright in the sky and the breeze against your skin caressed. Loss kept her awake too long into too many nights.

She shook her head to push away the thoughts, leaning her forehead against the cool glass of the rear passenger window. Eventually, they pulled up to her duplex, and she thanked the driver, scurrying out of the Ford and up the porch steps with a sense of relief.

Smokey, her short-haired grey cat, meowed at her as she opened the front door, standing at attention just a few feet away before turning in confidence toward the kitchen where his tins of food took up one of the cabinets. He paused after three steps and glanced back at Dee, meowing again until she took a step in his direction. Satisfied, he continued leading her to his food bowl.

"Ungrateful beast," she muttered, pulling him into her arms and feeling him stiffen. She cuddled him against her lips, listening to the purr he couldn't control as he not-so-patiently waited for Dee to set him down and put his food in his bowl.

She watched him eat on his salmon and white fish, the stench of the canned food no less offensive for being familiar and leaned her elbows against the cool marble countertop. Her mind filled with images of Tank again, with his thick muscles in all the right places and the dimples that showed when he unbent his stern expression to smile.

She sighed and pushed herself away from the counter and her thoughts. She didn't even know the man's full name, and he'd all but called her a kid. Was she legal, indeed! No sense woolgathering about a man she would never see again.

Speaking of men, Harley Jones could go down on that list as well. Dee had always harbored a secret dream of falling in love with a real-life cowboy. Maybe that's why she'd accepted the date with Harley, whom she'd met over the avocado bin at the grocery store. Well, that was the first and last time she went out with a total stranger, no matter that he was a rodeo star and had the championship belt buckle to prove it.

What she needed now was a shower, a long, hot steaming washing to bathe away the creepy feeling of being pawed by Harley in the middle of a bar and then further embarrassing herself by practically groping a man, the likes of which she'd never seen before, a wall of a man with lips that looked perfectly kissable.

"Really, Dee," she told herself, speaking aloud because most days her voice alone filled the air in her tiny duplex. "If Daddy only knew what you'd been up to and where your thoughts had wandered."

Her voice trailed off as she made her way down the hall to the bathroom. Truth be told, since she'd made the bold move to the big city, the daily calls with her father had dwindled. He stayed busy enough with the demands of his congregation, and Dee grew tired of hearing the tone of regret and fear in his voice, as if he had failed as a parent because his remaining child no longer wanted to live with him.

As she turned on the shower and undressed, she tried not to think about how different life might have been if her older brother and mother had not been taken from them. "Stop it," she commanded in a shaky voice, then stronger, like a drill sergeant, "STOP."

Smokey, sauntering toward the bathroom to beg for a drink from the tub, pitched his back into an arch and scurried into Dee's bedroom, banging into her dresser along the way before skittering under the bed. She could see his yellow eyes blinking at her from the shadows.

"You are such a cat," she told him, grateful for the distraction. She grabbed the shower cap from the hook on the back of the bathroom door and forcefully shoved her considerable length of hair into it, feeling some of the fine strands breaking away against the push of her fingers.

The damage somehow made her feel better, and she stepped into the tub and turned the water as hot as it would go, allowing the searing stings of the jet spray to redden her skin. More punishment.

Her father would tell her to pray, as he'd done for a long time now, ever since the day they'd stood in the pouring rain like a scene from a bad movie and watched two coffins being lowered into the ground.

Dee didn't pray anymore unless God counted a curse on her lips. Eventually, even cursing seemed silly. God had nursed her wounds when she'd been bullied as a child for her smallness and for the lisp she'd had to see a therapist to conquer. She had seen Him as a loving, kind creator for many years, a big man in a white robe who had a smile much like her daddy's. Because she couldn't conjure Him now without seeing some sort of monster, she'd long since given up believing in Him at all. That seemed easier than the alternative of trying to understand a god who supposedly loved her taking away the very beings who made her heart beat. Worse still, to go on living with a father who praised God as if losing everything was a blessing instead of a curse.

She flipped the water temperature so that the ice-cold sprays made her teeth chatter. When she finally turned off the water and stepped out of the tub, her limbs felt heavy and protested the effort it took to dry.

Pulling the shower cap from her head, she felt the weight of her hair as it slipped down past her buttocks, tickling her upper thighs. She should cut it. Studying her reflection in the mirror, her marred, splotchy skin, her green eyes hollow in her pale face, she thought how the hair, which she had not cut since that terrible day, was all that she had left of those she'd lost.

Every other cell in her body had changed over the past decade and more, but not the hair swinging down around her. She pulled up a handful and kissed the ends before smashing her face into the strands. This was the very same hair her mother had kissed that morning, the same hair her brother had tugged affectionately as they walked to the bus stop together.

"Aw, hell," she muttered, sucking back the tears that started to flow, knowing that sleep would allude her now. "Might as well find a good book."

She flipped on the bedroom light, glancing at Smokey perched on the end of the bed. He flipped his tail at her, then closed his eyes again. Slipping into her pajamas, she scanned the shelves of books lining one wall of her room, picked out a slasher horror and curled up in bed.

She'd had enough failed romance for one evening to spend the whole night reading some outrageous fairy tale, after all.

Chapter Three

Brother Thomas stood five-foot-seven in his stocking feet, with biceps and calves that bulged, and a sway to his gait from his days in the Navy. He'd grayed since Tank last saw him, that summer when he'd joined the Army and finally found a family. Stepping into the gym at the rec center that afternoon, Tank stood in the corner and watched as Thomas patiently explained to the scrawny little boy standing across from him on the mat the force from the hips that put the power into a punch. He chuckled when Thomas encouraged the kid to practice right into the center of his gut. For all the youth's scrawniness, anger packed the punch, all the horror of his young life vibrating in his thin arms. Thomas grunted, but he didn't flinch.

The older man noticed Tank then, tapping the youth on the shoulder and stepping off the mat, toward him. His grin, wide and toothy, revealing the gap between the older man's front teeth, made a place in the depths of Tank's belly, long forgotten, lurch. Thomas reached his long arms up and over Tank's shoulders, pulling him into the scents of peppermint and pipe smoke that always surrounded the man.

"My stars," he rumbled in Tank's ear. "Is it really little Tucker Brand standing before me?"

Tank slapped his hands against Thomas' shoulders in return before pulling away, moving his fingers to the other man's wide shoulders. "I was never little, Brother Thomas." He let his gaze move to the young man on the mats, who'd ignored the groups of boys clustered around the old gym, and now stood slouched against the basketball goal, his lower lip pushed out.

"He's even angrier than you were," Thomas said. "There's too much anger anymore."

Tank shrugged. "Plenty of reasons to be angry, especially at that age."

Thomas gave him a squinty stare that told him he should know better without saying anything. The older man motioned to the bleachers behind Tank and moved to sit down on the lowest bench. Tank sank onto the seat beside him, resting his elbows on his knees and lacing his fingers together. He studied his boots against the worn wood of the gym's floor.

"How's the retirement?" Thomas asked after a moment.

Tank grunted. "Practically threw me out on my ear."

Thomas jostled him. "You've had your twenty years. Don't you want to know what God has planned for you next?"

When Tank said nothing, only grunted again and glared at the older man out of the corner of his eye, Thomas chuckled. "Too soon, huh?" He watched the boys rough-housing on the mats, a few showing the practiced moves of defense he'd taught them, then stretched his legs in front of him, tapping his worn sneakers against each other.

Tank studied the sneakers tapping back and forth, the faded, red canvas with holes where once there'd been grommets, the white, rubber tips gray with wear. They might just be the same pair of sneakers Thomas had been wearing that summer afternoon a quarter century before when the policeman who'd nabbed Tank for trying to shoplift some chocolates from a convenience store hauled the defiant thirteen-year-old through the rec center's thick, wooden doors and told him he could spend his summer afternoons with the funny-looking man in his black t-shirt and loose, long shorts or spend its entirety in prison.

"What brings you here, Tucker?" Thomas asked finally, bringing Tank back to the present.

"Not pleased to see me?" Tank grinned, but he still cringed inside every time Thomas insisted on calling him Tucker. Only one other man had ever called him by that name, and he could not be more different than the one sitting next to Tank now.

Thomas snorted. "Got something better than silly questions?"

"Maybe," Tank told him, rising to his considerable height, "but not today." He pursed his lips and whistled loudly enough to catch the attention of all the boys in the gym. They looked at him with wary eyes not quite hardened enough to hide the little bits of hope beneath. "Get these mats up now," Tank ordered as if they were troops and not children. "Time for a game."

Cowards run. He remembered the first time he'd heard the words, sitting on the front stoop with blood dribbling down from his nose into his mouth so that he could taste the metallic tinge of his own fear. His father had barked the words at him, his spit flying in the hot, humid air, the words sounding like both a sentence and a curse.

Tank had been six, enjoying a lazy summer, fishing in the pond and playing sandlot baseball of an evening while the neighborhood men sit around sipping beers and swapping stories about war. That day, the boys who came to cause trouble were twice Tank's age and three times his size. They'd come around the corner, grabbing up little Nikki Trent and pounding on him.

Knowing that choosing to stay would be choosing to get pummeled as well, Tank turned on his heel and ran, hoping to get help. His father had given him the bum nose and the fat lip. Nikki's mother, her hair in curlers, her apron strings flapping in the wind, had grabbed two of the men standing around to go off and save her son while Tank stood and had the first of many tough lessons.

Neill Brand was a giant of a man, with hands the size of saucers and a jagged scar across his left eye that made him look more like a pirate than a truck driver running routes up the eastern coast. When he wasn't absent on long hauls, he sat on the porch stoop and watched the world sweep by around him, his black eyes flat, his hands always filled with bottles of beer and the cigarettes he rolled, his fingers always yellowed and cracked.

If Neill Brand loved, it was an elusive thing, like the way the old man let his wife, a thin, bird-like woman with eyes that darted and never settled, lay her fragile hand in the crook of his arm without slapping her against the nearest wall. He had served in the Marines for five long years and had three tattoos along his biceps that moved when he flexed, like dancing ladies on a stage. He never smiled except for when he had Tank scrunched in a corner, bleeding and bruised, learning another lesson in a world of dirt and mended shirts and cracks in the walls that let the winter wind blow ice onto the covers of the roll-out Tank called a bed.

Tank's mother worked as a hairdresser during Neil Brand's long hauls. They had some good, peaceful times then, with no worries about getting hit.

When Neil came home, well, peace became a memory. He expected Lilla Brand to wait on him hand and foot. A jealous man, his father would beat on his mother if another man so much as glanced in her direction. One reason among many why Lilla Brand kept to the house whenever Neil spent time there.

It probably would have gone on that way for the rest of Lilla's life, except Neil Brand had the good grace to get in a bar fight a thousand miles from home. His head hit the sharp edge of a table, killing him instantly.

Lilla never had another man after that. She worked all the time to keep a roof over her son's head and food in his belly. When Tank grew big enough, he helped too. She died the year before Tank graduated from high school.

∞ ∞ ∞

Thomas Moon never raised a hand in anger to anyone. Even in the Navy, he'd served in the galleys as kitchen assistant and finally cook. But he had a way about him, a look in his sky-blue eyes, layers to his silences, that made a boy think more about being good than had any of Neil Brand's fists.

When he decided to become a soldier, Tuck wanted Thomas Moon to hear the news first. Later, in those tough moments when Tank's heartbeat mingled with the rapid staccato of gunfire threatening his death, he pictured Thomas Moon, the only person in his world to give a damn.

Now, Tank, covered in sweat, took the towel Brother Thomas offered him and swiped at his face and neck. "Your brother still own that café around the corner?" he asked.

Thomas shook his head. "Sold it to a conglomerate a couple of years ago. But the café still makes the best pancakes in the state."

A few minutes later, Tank thought the new owners must have

spruced up the place as he glanced at the tables covered in old road maps and slick with the clear overlay of varnish sealing them in, at the red and black benches, upholstery free of nicks or marks, obviously new.

They sat at a booth with a table full of food between them before Thomas looked at him and asked point blank, "So, what's troubling you, son?"

Tank swallowed. "You know the story," he finally managed, a question more than a statement.

But Thomas just grunted, his silence forcing Tank to shift on the seat. The new vinyl creaked underneath him. "Nothing has been the same since Africa," he paused, glancing at the sugar dispenser, so new its silver lid gleamed. He missed the old, with the dents and smears of ketchup that gave them character.

It was the first time he'd said the words aloud, admitting his weakness to the one person in the world whom he could trust not to judge him for it. He felt the tightness in his chest loosen just a little bit.

"You were fortunate to do what you did for so many years without losing anyone," Thomas said in that quiet, calm voice that always seemed to cut through whatever emotions Tank had tumbling around, steadying him.

"Somehow, knowing that doesn't make it any easier." Tank drummed his fingers against the slick tabletop and closed his eyes briefly before continuing. He couldn't say this next bit and look his old mentor in the eyes. "Death was hard enough when it happened to the other side. When it happened to men I commanded. . . . If I had just aborted the mission," he let the words peter out, took a deep breath and opened his eyes.

Thomas' blue eyes pierced through him, peeling away Tank's layers like stripping the paint off a wall. "How are you keeping your time lately? You can't expect to sit back on your laurels and live off your pension."

"I haven't decided yet." The words forced themselves past Tank's tight lips. Truth be told, he had no clue what he might do. Twenty years in the Army had taught him many skills, most of which he could put to use in professions that might just as quickly put him back in a position to kill or be killed, worse yet, to place a subordinate in the line of fire. He couldn't handle another violent death on his conscience. But, what else was he qualified to do?

As if Thomas could read his mind, he grunted again before offering. "I could always use help at the center. You saw how those boys took to you this afternoon. It would give you something to do while you sort things out."

The idea appealed. Truth be told, playing basketball with the youths who reminded Tank so much of himself at that age, well it gave him time without feeling the weight of Africa bearing down on him. The more he considered, he realized that afternoon had given him the most peaceful one in memory.

Still, he hesitated to commit. He knew what afternoons with Brother Thomas would also bring, subtle nudging toward accountability, toward Tank's lapsed relationship with the loving God Thomas held so dear.

Sensing Tank's hesitation and probably the reason for it knowing Thomas, the older man shrugged his shoulders. "Think on it at least, Tucker. You know where to find me."

Thomas stood up then, reaching for his wallet to throw a bill on the table. When Tank moved to protest, the older man just shook his head. "I've got an appointment with young Sammy's mother," he said, explaining his abrupt departure. "The boy's having a rough time of it since his father got sent to the pen for drug trafficking. He really idolized the man."

He stopped abruptly, as if he realized he'd been thinking out loud with words that ought not be said in the middle of a public restaurant. He grinned at Tank and tapped him on the shoulder. "You know where to find me," he told him. And then, as he had been doing since that first meeting a quarter of a century before, he laid his hand on top of Tank's head and uttered his heartfelt benediction:

*"The LORD bless you and keep you; the LORD make his face shine upon you and be gracious to you; the LORD turn his face toward you and give you peace."**

*Numbers 6:24-26 (NIV)

Chapter Four

Her little VW Bug lurched to one side, and Dee just managed to pull onto the shoulder without causing an accident. She jumped out of her car and ran around to the passenger side. Sure enough, her front tire lay in shreds in front of her. She glanced at her watch. 5:30 already? Of course, today she'd wind up with a flat, when she had a blind date to meet in less than an hour and a desperate need to get home and change for it.

She went to the front of her vehicle and popped the hood, pulling out her bags of school supplies and papers to get to the spare and jack. It didn't occur to Dee that she'd never changed a tire before until she got what she thought was the jack out of the trunk and then tried to lift out the spare. The tire, though smaller than the ones already on the car, just didn't want to budge.

She was so busy concentrating on her task, she didn't hear the other vehicle stop behind her car or the approach of heavy boots on the pavement. So, when the deep voice offered from behind her, "Let me help you, darlin'," she practically jumped out of her skin, twisting in mid-air so that she fell back against and right into the open trunk of her car.

She rubbed at her now sore rear and looked up past her twill pants and ballerina flats to see a familiar giant towering over her. "Tank," she exclaimed, leaning back on her elbows as if she'd meant to lie back into her car all along. "What are you doing here?"

Tank reached forward and lifted Dee easily back onto her feet. He cocked his head and studied Dee with those amazing brown eyes before asking, "Do I know you, darlin'?"

Dee swallowed back her disappointment. Several weeks had passed since that disastrous "date" with Harley. "I guess it's just as well you can't remember," she told him. "It's nice to see you again, anyway."

He shrugged, then gave her a lopsided grin. "I can see now why your daddy calls your loose hair naughty. All pinned up like that, you look more like an angel."

Dee flashed Tank a brilliant smile. "You do remember. I'm so glad."

Tank chuckled and stepped beside Dee, reaching behind her to easily take the spare out of her trunk. He rounded the front of the car and practically lifted it by himself as he put the jack in place beneath it. "Don't ever go into covert ops, darlin'," he told her as he made quick work of changing out her flat. "I doubt you have a secret in the world you can keep."

If he only knew the secrets she kept, she thought absently as she moved to stand behind him and study what he did so that if she found herself in this predicament again, she'd be better prepared to help herself. Without thinking about it, she rested her hand on Tank's muscled shoulder. She took in a deep breath of his cologne and the woodsy smell that seemed to be a part of his skin. With an effort, Dee squelched the desire to run her fingers through his thick, tawny hair.

"You keep breathing down my neck like that, angel," Tank said suddenly, his voice low, "I'm liable to forget you plan on being a good girl."

Dee gave his shoulder a pat and stepped back. "Sorry," she said. "You smell better than the cool air after a summer rain, Tank."

He snorted. "Don't ever repeat that, angel," he ordered. "I've got a reputation to keep."

He stood up, wiped his hands on a rag he'd pulled from one of the cavernous pockets of his fatigue pants and easily placed the jack and flat back in her trunk, followed by the bags she'd set down on the pavement.

"This is the second time you've saved me from a predicament, Tank" Dee said as he closed the hood of her car. "You're going to have to let me do something nice for you some time. Maybe dinner. As a thanks."

He would refuse. In fact, his brown eyes darted around as if he were a deer in head lights. Before she could think too much about it, Dee stepped up onto his combat boots and grabbed a handful of the t-shirt he wore so she could look him straight in the eye. "Just say yes, Captain," she ordered.

Tank surprised a yelp out of her when he wrapped his arms around her waist and lifted her easily up against the solid wall of muscle that was his body. "I can think of more interesting ways for you to thank me, angel," he told her, his lips centimeters from her own.

Dee placed her palms firmly on his cheeks and smacked her lips against his playfully before pulling back in his grasp. "I think that would be much more interesting, too, believe it or not," she told him, "but I am a good girl, and I aim to remain one. So, how about dinner?"

Her hands were still on his cheeks so that when he smiled briefly, they moved in and out. He turned his lips into one palm and smacked her back before sitting her on the ground. "Okay, darlin'," he gave in, "sometime."

Now that she stood back on solid ground, literally, Dee wondered at her audacity. She felt lucky Tank hadn't taken possession of her lips and thrust his tongue down her throat, the way she behaved. The fact that she wondered exactly how Tank's tongue would taste inside her mouth made her blush from her neck up. She could feel the blush as it crawled to her hairline.

Suddenly, she remembered her blind date and grimaced, glancing at her watch. "I'm going to be so late," she muttered.

Tank snaked a finger under her chin and raised her eyes to meet his. He studied her face a long moment before asking in a gruff voice. "Late for what?"

Dee felt embarrassment snake around her lower neck and creep into her cheeks. He didn't need to know she had a date with a man she'd never met before. She pushed her back up straight and forced herself to look him in the eye. "I have a date."

Tank's easy smile hardened just a flicker before he shrugged. "Well, don't let me keep you, angel." He took a step toward his truck.

"Wait," Dee called out, then when he turned, "let me have your number, so I can invite you to dinner, sometime." She pulled out her phone and moved to hand it to him.

Tank studied her for a long moment before taking the phone from her outstretched hand and putting in his data. "Your date not going to mind his girl cooking for another guy?" he asked, his voice casual even though Dee noticed his shoulders stayed tight.

"I said I had a date," Dee corrected. "I never said anything about having a boyfriend."

"And you're going to be late," he said, handing her the phone, studying her with an expression that read everything, even her soul. He grinned suddenly, "Do you even know what he looks like, angel?"

Dee cleared her throat. How did he know? She looked down at her ballerina flats and scuffed them in the gravel on the side of the road before admitting, "According to my coworker, he's the cutest cousin she's got."

She shrugged and forced herself to look up at him then, dreading the pity she'd see in his all-knowing eyes. Instead of pity, or worse yet disgust, Tank looked at her with those same probing eyes as if he wanted to figure out a deep puzzle.

"Why aren't you married, darling? Something wrong with the boys your age?"

Yes, she thought. They always seemed to want more from her than she felt capable of giving, both emotionally and physically. She told Tank, "I have dates. I date plenty. I just don't have a particular boyfriend."

He crossed his arms in front of his chest. "People who date plenty don't usually need to endure a blind date," he challenged.

Dee rolled her eyes. "Since you witnessed the results of my last date, pardon me for trying something new."

Tank looked out toward the pasture beyond the side of the road, where an abandoned shack leaned against the wind, its wooden boards slanted and gapped like imperfect teeth. She could see his pulse ticking along his jaw. He moved to the passenger side of his truck and opened the door.

"Hop in, angel."

Dee willed her feet to remain planted, even as her toes wriggled in her flats. A rain drop, fat and slick, flopped onto the top of her head and slid down the side of her cheek. Startled, she glanced overhead to see a thunderous cloud lurking just behind her.

She opened her mouth to argue against Tank's arrogant tone and bullying manner, but then a second and third raindrop, each bigger than the last, splashed against her arm and left cheek. Before she could think too much about it and change her mind, she skipped toward the open door and let Tank help her inside the cab.

By the time he made his way around to the driver side of the truck and seated himself behind the steering wheel, his t-shirt clung to his muscles, splattered in ugly globs. Tank watched as Dee looked out on the rain, coming down in great sheets now that pounded on the roof above them and filled the quiet. She glanced at her watch and back out at the storm.

"I'm never going to make it in time for Jason," she muttered.

Tank turned the key in the ignition, which roared to life, filling the space in the sudden silence between them. When he had pulled up behind a stranded motorist, the last person he'd expected to see was this little sprite of a woman. Funny how that encounter seemed like a lifetime ago, even though only a few weeks had passed since then.

In that time, Tank kept meeting with Brother Thomas and his band of troubled youths, including having long talks with Thomas into the wee hours of the night. He'd also decided that instead of being in a job where he might have to take a life, he'd rather be in a position where he might save one. He'd been coming home from signing up for EMT training when he'd seen Dee's car.

Glancing out the side mirror to check for traffic, he pulled back out onto the road and watched in the rearview mirror as the rain folded in on her VW and faded from sight. He cut his eyes to the right, scanning Dee as she sat so prettily beside him, her hands folded in her lap.

Even in her work clothes, Dee appealed to him. He shook himself mentally. He'd only hurt a nice girl like Dee, a preacher's daughter on top of everything else that was sweet and petite about her. Still, he wasn't about to let her go on a blind date. He told himself he just wanted to protect her from all those men out there who might take advantage of her, but his gut knew better.

Just as he started to tell his gut to shut up, Dee reached across the space between them and grabbed his arm, exclaiming, "Hey, where are we going?"

That touch affected him more than he cared to admit, like those sweet lips of hers smacking against his as if she had never really kissed a man before. He forced a grimace to his face.

"Well, darling, you look hungry," he said, glancing toward her, making sure she felt more curious than startled.

She let go of his arm and crossed hers in front of her chest, settling back into the seat cushion. "I have plans for dinner." She looked at her watch again and made a noise. "I had dinner plans."

"You still do," Tank assured her.

"I don't even have his number," Dee said, as if he hadn't spoken. "He'll think I saw him and changed my mind or something."

Tank found himself getting irritated. "Enough about the blind date that was," he told her. "What do you like to eat?"

"Is this a date?" she asked, irritation mixed with a teasing tone. "Because I was really counting on having a date this evening."

"And anyone will do?" Tank stopped at a red light and shifted in his seat so he could turn in her direction.

She looked at him, and her eyes seemed to hide a worldliness he wouldn't have credited to her, a kind of sadness that made him want to know more. "I think we both know you're not just anyone," she told him, her voice brisk and a little far away.

The light turned green, pulling Tank's eyes back to the road. Just as well. She brought out a protective instinct in him that Tank didn't understand and would rather avoid. The rain began to dissipate as he drove into the parking lot of a popular Tex-Mex restaurant. Even though the usual hour had long since passed, the lot remained fairly full.

"I love this place," Dee said as he pulled into a space and shut off the truck's engine.

He helped her out of the truck and would have settled for walking beside her into the restaurant except she slipped her hand around his arm and pulled it into her body, hurrying her strides to keep up with his long ones. He tried to ignore the tingles of sensation even the simple contact made.

Once they settled at a table and ordered, Tank studied Dee

across the table, the way she smiled with her whole face and yet her eyes darted around the room nervously. She reminded him of himself, how unsettled he felt after losing men he commanded, no matter that no one officially blamed him.

He took a long drink of the iced tea the waitress brought to the table to change the turn of his disturbing thoughts. Most of the women he'd ever dated kept up a steady stream of conversation without really waiting for or caring about Tank's response. But Dee, with her arms resting easily on top of the table, merely seemed content to wait on Tank to begin any further conversation between them. A warm feeling spread through him with a surprisingly-calming effect.

Suddenly, Dee yawned, holding a palm over her mouth and apologizing after. Tank chuckled. "Little tykes keep you busy today, did they?" he asked.

She shrugged. "It was a long week. I have this one student, Jimmy. He's the cutest little red-head, complete with the button nose and freckles sprinkled across his cheeks. But he can't stay still to save his life. I turn to write on the blackboard, and he jumps up from his desk to do a little dance. He bounces pencils off the top of his desk. Most weeks, I can handle him, but he was really something this week. He wore me out."

He didn't know exactly why he'd insisted on taking her to dinner, but he certainly enjoyed the view of her sitting across from him, with her creamy skin and brilliant eyes and that halo of golden hair. Something about Dee reminded him of a dark-haired beauty he'd met in the Middle East during his second tour of duty. He'd actually come close to considering a long-term commitment with that one.

"You never did tell me what you do for a living," she said, twining her fingers under her chin, bringing Tank back to the moment.

He took another gulp of tea before answering, "I'm retired."

"Retired?" she exclaimed with such force, her twined braids bounced. "Impossible."

Tank grinned. "I'm an old snake eater, darlin'," he said, using the term for a Special Forces member. "Twenty years in the army."

"How long have you been retired? Any plans for your next career?"

"I was just heading back from signing up for an EMT course when I saw you stranded on the side of the road."

"So, were you a medic in the army?"

Tank held back a smile. "No, not a medic."

She cocked her head. "Is this one of those, 'I'd tell you, but I'd have to kill you' situations?"

He did grin then. "Something like that."

Their food arrived. Dee took a bite of her cheese enchiladas and groaned. "This is so delicious."

"I thought you'd be the type to eat like a bird," he told her.

She laughed. "Oh, no. I love food. Thank goodness I have a fast metabolism. What made you interested in EMT training?"

The question made Tank uncomfortable. He shifted in his seat and rubbed the back of his neck. "Something different, I guess," he finally answered.

Dee cocked her head. He had a funny feeling that she saw right through his equivocation. Instead of calling him on it, she merely nodded, "M-m-kay."

They ate in silence after that. When they finished, Tank looked out where the dark had descended. "Time to get you home, darlin'."

She nodded. "Let me pay for supper. It's the least I can do, for all the help."

Tank pulled his wallet out of his back pocket. "Don't think so."

Dee scrunched her nose. "I can tell it's no use arguing with you."

They got in the truck and headed back to Dee's car. Tank put the truck into park and came around to open her door. "I'll follow you to your house," he ordered, "and make sure you don't have any other issues. You'll need to get that tire fixed ASAP."

She saluted him and winked. "Yes, Captain."

He followed her to a small duplex, white brick with red doors and shutters. He knew which side belonged to Dee with its big wreath of sunflowers on the door and rocking chair on one side. Putting the truck into park, he stepped out just as Dee popped open her hood to gather up her tote bag with its school supplies.

"You've got to come over for supper soon," she told him.

Standing in the moonlight, she looked like a China doll, fragile and in need of protection. Tank felt his stomach clench. He was out of the protection business.

"Give cousin Jason a chance, angel," he told her, leaning in to place his lips against her smooth cheek. He heard her sharp intake of breath and smiled against her skin.

Without saying another word, he got back in his truck, starting it with a quick jerk on the ignition. She stood like a statue for several moments before it dawned on her that he planned to wait until she entered her house before taking off. With a little sigh, she turned and made her way inside the duplex.

Tank pulled away from the curb and gunned his truck, running from something, stiff with the intuition that he could not run from himself.

Chapter Five

The call signs crackled over the radio, then cut dead. Tank felt the sweat pouring down the back of his shirt, under his flak jacket. He could hear the quick intake of breath from men on either side of him. Somewhere behind, one of the women they came to rescue whimpered quietly. One of the other women, whose panicked screaming would have gotten them all killed, lay in a heap just where Jackson had decked her.

His unit had begun this mission just hours before. Tribes in this inner-most section of the African veldt had joined together briefly to attempt a coup against their latest dictator. But too soon, the tribes turned back on each other, so that bodies piled up like cordwood in every village they passed.

Tank and his men had the task of dropping into the heart of the conflict to save a group of American missionaries who ran an Eswatini orphanage. The mission seemed jinxed from the beginning. Two of Tank's best men didn't even make the cargo plane for the flight across the ocean. Sims, Tank's best tracker, had broken his leg while showing a new recruit some pointers about the latest obstacle course on their fitness track. Lee, the youngest recruit, failed his latest physical when the doctor detected a never-before-diagnosed murmur.

That left Tank with only eight highly-trained soldiers to safely extract more than a dozen men, women and even two young children from a territory that would be hard to trek under the best of circumstances. Now, besides dodging poisonous reptiles, hungry wildlife, and twenty miles of open desert on foot in the dead of night in order to reach the extraction point, Tank's ragtag team also faced the dangers of the constant exchange of machine gun fire and RPG blasts all around them.

It was the heat of the long day, with the sun beating directly down on them as they huddled behind a thick copse of underbrush, the missionaries huddled in a circle in the middle of the perimeter set by his men. The dead radio was just another in a long line of tragedies this mission, but one that could be fatal. The last message seemed to say the extraction point had been compromised.

Tank wiped the sweat from his eyes and glanced at his sergeant, Barry, a wiry red-head who stood five-foot-ten in his stocking feet but who could beat a man within an inch of his life twice his size and not break a sweat. Tank had seen it with his own eyes more than once. "Can you fix that d--- radio?" Tank hissed in a low voice, not wanting to alert the enemy or the nervous Christians huddled behind him. Not for the first time this mission, he squelched the urge to mock them about the power of their prayers to their God.

Barry licked his lips, but even his tongue was dry in this desert heat, and all he managed was to move the dead, flaky skin from one side of his mouth to another. "I think that last bullet through the casing cracked the transistor."

"Well, get the medic kit and use the liquid bandaid if you have to, just get it fixed." Tank didn't say the rest of it, that if the sergeant failed, they could all die. The grim set to the sergeant's usually jovial expression told Tank he already knew.

Leaving Barry to his pack-rat devices, Tank shuffled over to the oldest member of his team other than himself, keeping his body tight and low to avoid being seen by the snipers guarding the outskirts of the village where they had hoped to bed down during the heat of the day before making what would be the last, mad dash to safety.

Whitey, lifetime army, had been demoted so many times, he no longer worried with anything that didn't involve absolute life or death. When Tank reached him, he had out his non-regulation Bowie knife, cleaning out from under his fingernails with the deadly-looking blade. He didn't even look up when Tank neared him, coming to a stop when his knees grazed the other man's.

"We've got maybe two hours before that boy on the south flank gets tired of just sitting and makes his way over here to blow our cover," Whitey said without preamble. He spit into the dirt beside him, managing a considerable loogy when all Tank could taste inside his dry mouth was the blood from his cracked lips. "We're gonna have to move, Cap." He glanced back at the women and especially the two children clinging to their mother's torn, dusty skirt. "We're not all gonna make it, either."

Tank bit down on his tongue, drawing even more blood. As team captain, it was his decision alone on how they proceeded. He knew Whitey was right, but it didn't make his choices any easier. "They might keep the men as leverage," he said, thinking out loud.

Whitey gave him a sidelong scowl. "Some of those women can't trek another mile, much less ten," he reminded Tank. "I can carry two of the skinnier ones, maybe strap a kid to my back, but even you couldn't manage that water buffalo who can't seem to stop bawling anyway. We've still got to be able to fire a gun, Tank."

"Let us go as far as we can with you," a quiet voice said from behind them. Tank turned to see one of the leaders of the missionary group, a tall, skinny man with drooped shoulders and a peaceful smile. "If we cannot keep up with the rest of you, that is for God to decide. None of us want you to die trying to save us." He smiled, but the sadness didn't leave his eyes. "And, please, no more killing because of us."

Tank blew out a hot breath. "You want us to just lay down our arms and let them execute us like Christ on the cross, mister?" he scoffed. "We don't do that sh--, brother. We aren't trained that way."

Barry scurried up next to Tank, cutting off whatever other useless thing the missionary might have to say. "I got her working again, Cap," he explained, waving his mic in the air in front of him. "Extraction points been moved to two miles south of us. In two hours."

He pointed, and Tank let out another frustrated sigh. Between his rag-tag group and extraction lay the nearby village streaming with soldiers and guns as well as a croc-infested watering hole they'd have to wade through with no time to go around. "Piece of cake," he told Barry, his lips forming a smirk. He glanced back at the missionary and snarled. "Think your God can conjure up a Red Sea kind of miracle, preacher? We're going to need all the help we can get."

When the man acted as if he were about to begin praying right away, Tank yanked him none too gently by the arm and shook him. "No time for that now, preacher," he hissed in the man's ear. "I want you men around the women and children. Shield them with your bodies if you have to. Stay low and stay close together. Can you do that?"

The man's face turned even more sallow but he nodded. "We have to."

Tank and his men pulled into a tight cluster as Tank signaled his orders. They checked their remaining ammunition with grim faces and readied for imminent assault. Barry made one last contact with the command post before Tank gave the order to move forward, no turning back.

The first fatality happened suddenly, unexpectedly, as one of his men moved to help one of the missionaries who'd stumbled and stepped right into the oncoming bullet from a rifleman perched yards away, just outside the gathering well for the village. The soldier spun sideways and crumpled to the ground, a hole the size of a softball where his heart should be.

Tank knew better than to feel anything then. He scooped down and shifted the dead weight onto his shoulders fireman-carry style and urged his charges left where the earth fell off into a gully. They slid down the embankment, leaving a trail of Ingram's blood as they went, and huddled at the bottom as bullets made whizzing noises over their heads.

"Nobody else is dying here today," Tank barked, an order, his voice low but sharp under the roar of the artillery. "Lincoln, set up that RPG and blow that village to hell. The rest of you be ready to run like the devil is on your tail."

Barry pulled up beside Tank, his breathing quick and hard and too loud in Tank's ears. "You can't carry Ingram the rest of the way, Cap," he stuttered. "These women and kids can't keep up forever."

"I'll worry about that when we get there," Tank barked, shifting Ingram's heavy body into a more comfortable hold on his shoulder. "Now, shut the f--- up and do your job, Barry. Tell them we're coming in hot."

An explosion rocked the air around them, sending a spray of sand that allowed for a smokescreen of cover. Tank rose up on the balls of his feet and started climbing, knowing that his men would follow. He heard them as they pushed the missionaries up and over the cliff, as the women wailed and the soldiers cursed at the top of their lungs. Then, all he could hear was the pounding in his ears of his feet hitting the sand as he rushed forward, spreading a wide swath of bullets from his automatic rifle as he went, grabbing the grenade from Ingram's belt and tossing it toward a cloud of approaching sand that could only be the enemy at one point.

They reached the watering hole like a lazy "s" curving toward the water. Two more of his men, Scott and Reynolds, were missing, along with two of the men and one of the women they should be rescuing. Tank turned to Barry who shook his head, which oozed blood that dripped from his pointy chin.

Tank swallowed hard and took a quick inventory of his remaining force. He was too many men down with too many civilians to save to worry about retrieving any more bodies, at least not yet. He made a silent vow to turn back from the chopper the minute he had the missionaries on board to return for his men and then made himself concentrate on the watering hole they'd yet to cross.

Forming his remaining five guys into a perimeter net, he started them across the murky water. Whitey laid out covering fire around them, warding off any hungry crocodiles. The two kids, a boy and a girl, bobbed on the shoulders of two of the men of the cloth, their eyes wide with fright, their little hands in death grips on the men's heads. *How could they believe in God after this mess*, Tank wondered.

It took them another half hour to wind their way through the scant cover between them and their destination, but finally the chopper's whirling blades sounded above the popping of the gunfire being exchanged all around them. Tank loaded the chopper, handing the shaking men and women up into the craft.

His own team stood outside with him, breathing hard, watching the ground more than each other. They had begun as eight. Now five stood flexing tired muscles.

Tank motioned for the flight crew to take off and turned to head back into the fire fight, determined to gather the bodies of his fallen men. The rest of his team poised to follow. Suddenly, a large hand clamped over Tank's shoulder and pulled him back into the hot metal of the bird. He looked up into the set mouth of his commanding officer, the man's hard face etched in fury.

"Get you and your men into this bird now, Captain," he barked. "That's an order."

When Tank moved as if to disobey, the hand clamped down even harder. "I'll shoot you myself, m---f----. It's too hot here. We'll have eight bodies instead of three. Now, move."

Tank felt every cell in his body rebel against the commander's harsh words, but he gave a quick nod to his team and waited as they piled into the chopper. When the last man, Whitey, had pulled himself up, Tank reluctantly took the older man's offered hand and jumped aboard.

The ride out of the desert, silent, the only noise the prayers of the missionaries and the whimpers of the children as the shock began to wane. Whitey sat down beside Tank and leaned into him. "No one could have done better," was all he said.

It was probably the best compliment anyone had ever given Tank, but it was cold, cold comfort. He knew one thing, if there was a God and Tank ever got anywhere near that cruel divinity, he better make sure he got a running start because Tank was going to beat the living hell out of him.

Chapter Six

Dee moved about her day listlessly, worn. The night before, Tank made it painfully clear he had no interest in going out with her. He seemed like the type of guy who had women. He wouldn't want to date a girl who planned on staying chaste, holding on to the fantasy of a happy ending, she reasoned. But the reasoning offered little comfort.

Why shouldn't she give herself to someone like Tank, all worldly-wise and built like a hero on the cover of a romance novel? Her daddy's eyes flashed in front of her, how they looked that ugly day when they covered Mama and Bobby in dirt. He'd started looking at Dee that way when he thought she wouldn't notice, his wayward daughter with a drawer full of crosses and Bibles she never opened, just kept there to curse when the pain in her chest had nowhere else to go.

"What happened to you last night?" Lisa McKenzie said, drawing Dee back to the moment and the limp Hot Pocket on her lunch plate.

She felt the color rise into her cheeks. "Is your cousin really mad? I didn't have any way of calling him."

Lisa sat down beside her and deadpanned, "You could have called me."

"Is it hot in here?" Dee blurted. Her shoulders fell. "I owe you and Jason an apology. I got distracted."

"Distracted how?" Lisa studied Dee with squinted eyes. "It was some other man," she accused.

"I got a flat. Then, the guy who stopped to help me with it turned out to be the guy from the bar last week. Before I knew what was going on, I was in his truck headed to a restaurant."

"The guy from the bar? That gropey cowboy?"

Dee rolled her shoulders. "Not him, the other one, the Army guy."

"Tell all," Lisa encouraged her, Cousin Jason seemingly forgotten.

"There's not much to tell, unfortunately. I don't think Tank will be seeing me again."

Lisa patted her back. "Jason's still interested. This time, I'll give you his number."

Dee worked up a smile. "Thanks. I'll call him and apologize about last night."

Her friend patted her arm. "Just don't mention Army guy, hm?"

The day shifted in on itself as the hours dragged by. Dee chased Jimmy around the classroom with a little more empathy, feeling just as itchy in her own skin. She gladly packed up her papers at the end of the day and headed home. When she got out of the VW at the duplex, she noticed her spare still on the car. It sent a stab of pain through her chest.

Making her way into her duplex, through the living room and little kitchen, she gave Smokey, curled up in the kitchen window, a sympathetic glance before opening the back door and stepping out on the little porch where she had her favorite rocking chair and a good book.

But once she got settled into her chair, she couldn't come up with the interest to read the latest thriller. Instead, her mind wandered where it shouldn't go, back to that day she turned 16 and ruined her family's lives forever.

Laying her head back against the top of the chair, she closed her eyes, breathing shallowly and waiting for the images to begin. They came in flashes, like a pile of cards being flipped through someone's fingers: Dee begging to take her first driving lesson; Bobby teasing her from the backseat of the family station wagon; Dee exchanging words with him, even after Mama told her to behave; Mama's screams ringing in Dee's ears long after the fire department pried her dead body from the passenger seat of the car; Bobby's eyes, wide open, unlike his mouth, pursed and tense, dying without a sound.

A warm hand closed around her upper arm, giving her a gentle, but persistent shake. She moaned slightly before jerking her eyes open. They widened when she saw who stood in front of her.

"Tank," she exclaimed, then swallowed, wishing she could take back the embarrassing enthusiasm of her greeting.

His brown eyes bore into her. She thought he might be reading her whole life story just looking at her. Instead of saying anything about it, he simply pushed her hair away from her forehead. His thumb and forefinger wrapped around her chin, lifting her gaze to his.

"Want a beer?" he asked.

"I-I don't have any," she stuttered out. She shook her head.

"What are you doing here?"

He ignored her question, releasing his hold on her and standing up straight. "We could go to the bar," he mumbled, rubbing his chin.

Dee felt her nerve endings come alive, climbing out of the sluggish stew of her memories. "Stop carrying on about drinking," she demanded, slapping her hand on the arm of the rocker. "I thought you told me to date someone else."

He looked toward the horizon before turning to face her again. "Neither one of us is much suited for relationships," he said.

She swallowed back a bulge in her throat. "Two broken people don't exactly make a whole," she agreed as it dawned on her why she felt this pull toward this man. Something haunted him, too. She could see the shadow of it dogging his steps.

"You still have that spare on your VW," he said after a minute. "I could get that fixed for you tomorrow."

"You're confusing me," she said.

"Angel, I'm confusing myself."

"To the showers now," Tank ordered, watching the ragtag team of boys he'd coached all afternoon as they bounced out of the gym and into the locker room, amazing him with their level of energy despite how hard he'd worked them. He glanced down at his sweat-soaked shirt. The hard work with the boys felt good, almost like being back on duty again.

"They enjoy having you here," Brother Thomas said, walking up beside Tank, crossing his arms over his chest and following Tank's gaze. "You look like you're carrying the weight of the world on your shoulders."

He shrugged, "I can't shake it."

Thomas reached across the distance between them, laying a heavy grip on Tank's shoulder. He stood like that for several, long moments. "You know what I'm going to say, Tucker."

He grunted, "Say it anyway."

"You will never shake it until you give it to the only One with the strength to bear it."

Tank stubbed his toe against the floor, watching it as if all the answers of the world might be found there. "How do you know?" he asked.

"He died on the cross, bearing the sins of all humanity. He has shoulders wide enough for your troubles, but you have to be willing to let them go. He can't take the burden from you if you haven't surrendered all to Him, including your need for control."

"You know me so well," Tank said, again looking down at his gym shoes, plain, canvas sneakers he'd picked up at a thrift store. "I've had to be in control of my men, of our situation."

"But you also had to be ready for the unexpected. Isn't that what happened in Africa?"

Tank took a few steps to the edge of the gym, picked up a towel, and wiped the sweat from his face and arms. Out of nowhere, Brother Thomas threw a basketball straight at Tank's stomach, right from the angle of his blind spot. Maybe this explained how it popped into him with a force that caused an oomph to escape his lips. But if he were being honest with himself, the real reason the basketball hit him, then bounced away until it dribbled and rolled to an anticlimactic stop several feet away, had emerald eyes and long, blonde hair.

As Tank watched, Brother Thomas retrieved the basketball, then walked over to him with it in his hands, held low over his abdomen. He just stood there in front of Tank then, who felt the pressure of the silence between them.

"There's another thing," Tank admitted, finally. "It's a woman."

Thomas made a noise in his throat before nodding slowly, recovering himself. "Is she married?" he asked, flicking an invisible piece of lint from his gym sweats, keeping his voice light.

Tank gave him a sideways glance. "No," he said, his voice flat.

Brother Thomas nodded. A series of quick questions and answers followed:

"Dating someone else?"

"No."

"Blessed with children?"

"No."

"Has two heads?"

"Be serious. She's got looks and personality, the whole package. Nothing about her is a problem."

"So, why are you afraid?"

Tank wanted to deny any fear, but instead the words came tumbling out of him. "How do I tell her the deepest parts of me, those darkest parts, and expect her to want me, let alone trust me? Pops, she's not a now and then girl, she's the marrying kind of woman. That's just not me."

"But you can't stop thinking about her. I can see it in your eyes, son. You deserve love as much as the next person. Did you ever stop to think that your pain might lessen if you shared it?"

That last question must be why Tank found himself in his truck after a shower, headed for Dee's little duplex. It sent him looking around the back of the house when he heard her rocking chair moving back and forth. It explained why he now pulled into a parking space at the Tex-Mex restaurant with Dee in the passenger seat.

She'd had her arms crossed the entire drive there, ever since she'd agreed to join him, though with obvious reluctance. Turning to face him now before they exited the truck, she tapped her forefinger against her arm.

"So, just to be clear here, is this a date, as in an event that will lead to other dates? You're not going to feed me again and disappear on me?"

Tank felt his jaw tighten. He didn't like anyone questioning his integrity. But then her wide eyes caught a sparkle off the neon light shining through the windshield, and he almost forgot her question. "Roger that," he finally managed, leaning across the distance between them and touching his lips to the tip of her nose. He felt proud of his restraint, considering he'd rather lay her out in the bed of the truck and make love to her under the stars.

Dee blinked rapidly when he leaned back against the driver's seat. He chuckled, "Do you want to go in?"

"What?" She shook her head as if to clear it. Maybe he wasn't the only one using restraint. "The restaurant. Of course. I'm starving all of a sudden."

"So am I," Tank agreed, opening his door and going around the front of the truck to let her out like a gentleman. When he had her hand in his, he faced them toward the brightly-painted stucco building, squeezing her fingers. "'Course, Tex-Mex isn't exactly what I'm hungry for."

Dee missed a step before clearing her throat and telling him in a truly innocent voice, too innocent to be real. "Jerry's Steakhouse is just up the road if you'd prefer."

He glanced down to see a big smile cover her face. She winked at him and squeezed his fingers back. "I'm trying to be good, remember?" Tank reminded her.

∞ ∞ ∞

Dee nodded solemnly because wasn't she trying to be good, too? A silly voice in the back of her mind mocked, why are you trying to be good? She shook her head to clear the thoughts. Walking into the restaurant, she felt as if her steps were on fragile ground. Tank might have his fingers locked with hers, but he looked as if he might bolt any moment.

She could relate. The closer she got to anyone, the greater her fear that they would see the real Dee, the one deep down inside all bruised and broken and unworthy of love. And this flutter in her chest every time Tank came near? It felt like she could easily fall deeply for him, that he could potentially see everything about her. He'd be gone forever then.

She shifted uncomfortably in her seat. Tank sat across from her studying the menu. She took the moment to watch his eyes flit across the pages. They were beautiful eyes, nothing like she'd ever seen before. He glanced up, catching her open adoration, and raised one bushy eyebrow.

Dee grinned. "I feel much too comfortable around you," she told him.

"You make that sound like a bad thing."

She nodded. "No telling what I might blurt out. My mouth moves faster than my thoughts, I warn you."

He wrapped one of her curls, loosely framing her face with the rest of her mass of hair pulled back, around his finger. "I like listening to your voice, darling. I never know what you're going to say."

She laughed. "Neither do I."

"DeAnna?" the familiar voice floated above her head, making the hairs along her arms stand on end.

She felt all the blood drain from her face as she turned slightly, looking up. He looked older than the last time, more grey in his hair, especially in his neatly-clipped beard. She licked her lips, which had gone dry as the desert, and continued looking at him.

"I'm sorry," Tank's voice penetrated the fog, sounding sharp, a warning. "Does she know you, mister?"

Dee's father gave Tank his polite-company grin, that patient smile that made her skin feel tight. "Randolph Culperson," he said in greeting, extending his hand.

Tank, making the quick connection upon hearing her surname, shook it, his hard lines softening. "Sir."

Randolph turned to look at her then. "I wasn't expecting to see you," he said, and she bit back a wave of disappointment, wondering how many times he'd come to the city without checking in on her.

She shrugged her shoulders, though it was difficult, considering how stiff they felt. "I guess you're wishing you'd gone with Chinese for dinner," she joked.

"Of course, I'm glad to see my only daughter," Randolph said, ignoring her sarcasm. Her father sat down on the bench seat beside her, forcing her to scoot to the far corner, practically climbing the wall to keep from touching him.

Tank glanced between father and daughter with a quizzical look on his face, but that knowing gleam, too, and he didn't say a word. Dee felt her cheeks burn. She sucked her lower lip between her teeth and bit down. Randolph gave her a sharp look.

"I only have a few minutes," Randolph said, his voice sounding a little less sure, almost apologetic.

"Dee says you're a preacher," Tank offered when Dee remained silent.

Her father turned to look at the man across from him. They exchanged a steady gaze. "I don't believe you said your name," Randolph said.

"Tucker Brand, sir."

"Brand. I don't believe I've ever met a Brand before." He tapped his fingers on top of the table, looking past Tank toward the back of the restaurant. Dee saw the group of serious-looking men then. He was probably here to meet with a group of preachers.

"How are your students?"

The question startled her. Dee swallowed. "Darling as ever," she managed.

"Good, good," he said, but Dee could tell his mind had already set on the group, away from her and this chance meeting that had spoiled her evening. Resentment boiled in her chest, fueling her need to assuage the guilt she felt when she was in her father's presence. She'd robbed him of his family, after all, no matter that she lost loved ones, too.

"Don't let us keep you," Dee blurted.

Her father started, then really looked at her. He reached out and lightly touched her hair. "Just like your mother's," he murmured, slicing her. Before she could think better of it, she reached up and grasped his hand in hers.

"I'm sorry, Daddy," she said.

"Come and visit soon," he said, ignoring her apology. He turned to Tank. "Mr. Brand."

He stood, stuffing his hands in his pockets. He looked between Tank and Dee, then nodded once as if deciding something before turning his back on them and strolling away. Dee felt her bones go limp. She laid her head against the wall beside her.

"What were you apologizing for?" Tank asked.

She jumped, as if she'd forgotten he was sitting there. "We don't get along very well ever since, well ever since I was a teenager," she told him. "I," she stopped, running her palm along the tabletop.

Tank reached across, laying his fingers on top of her hands to stop them. "You don't have to say any more, darling."

Dee's eyes followed Randolph as he sat at the table, his shoulders relaxed now, his conversation flowing easily. For just a moment, she allowed herself to wish for a closer relationship with him, a normal father-daughter bond, the one she didn't deserve. She turned back to Tank, who studied her with eyes that seemed to see everything, deep in her bones.

"I know how awkward that was," she started again, licking her dry lips. She should tell Tank the truth about herself, but she wanted more time with him.

"Awkward?" he shook his head. "Hell, if my old man walked in here, I'd knock him out cold, pay him back for some of those undeserved beatings I got as a kid."

"Well, it's not his fault. My father never raised a hand to me, not even when I," she stopped. "Your father beat you?"

"I've lived through worse things." Tank's fingers tapped on the table. His eyes drifted far away, and the nerve in his jaw twitched. Dee had a haunting sense that she knew the meaning of that look.

But instead of sharing her thoughts, Dee forced a smile to her lips and a lightness to her voice. "Well, there's no need to dwell on the past. I'd rather be here in the present with you."

The smile Tank gave Dee then melted her to her toes. She still had that warm feeling in her belly several hours later when she said good-bye to Tank in the truck to avoid the temptation of kissing him at her front door and wanting to invite him in. The fire in her blood turned to ice in her veins, though, when she spotted her father sitting in the rocking chair she had on the porch.

"Daddy," she said in a surprisingly steady voice, though her feet stumbled slightly beneath her.

He pushed his hands against the rocker arms to stand. "Hello, Bud."

The use of the old nickname should have touched her heart. Instead, it felt like picking at a scab on an old wound. She straightened her back. "What if I had gone home with Tank? Did you plan to sleep on my porch all night?" she asked boldly.

"If only I could give you the ability to forgive yourself," he said, ignoring her questions. "I wouldn't mind a cup of tea, Bud. I'm feeling the cold these days."

Dee swallowed the lump in her throat. She walked up the steps, pulling her keys from the little purse that matched her outfit, a splurge that suddenly felt like a leaden weight in her hand. "I think I have some Lipton's in the back of the pantry. I can't say how fresh it will taste."

"I'm sure it will be just fine," Randolph assured her, following closely behind as she stepped into her little duplex and flipped on the light. Her father's words echoed in her brain as he followed her into the kitchen and watched quietly as she prepared him a cup of tea.

Smokey came out of the bedroom, arcing his back when he

noticed the stranger in their midst. The grey cat hissed at Dee's father before scampering back into the safety of the dark hall.

"Cats never did like me," Randolph observed, leaning back in the kitchen chair so that it squeaked with the weight of him. "So it's Tank is it? I thought he looked like a military man."

"Retired. He's training to be an EMT now."

He took a sip of the tea, declaring, "Not so stale after all."

Dee sat down across from him because her muscles wouldn't hold her up anymore. She moved her hands across the tabletop. "You're wrong, about forgiveness. We both know it doesn't change a damn thing. They'll," she swallowed before she managed, "still be dead."

"Deanna," he said, his voice sharp, raw. He paused, seeming to draw in on himself, before continuing. "Forgiveness isn't about your mother or Mark. It's about you, being part of the living again."

"I'm part of the living."

Randolph straightened in the chair. "You know I mean the living water, the everlasting life that comes with trusting Jesus as your savior. You've turned your back on that truth for long enough."

"The only truth I know is death."

"I hardly think that proves your point. More like it supports mine."

Dee threw her hands to her cheeks in frustration. "Brow beating me won't make me change my mind," she blurted.

Randolph put his hands in the air. "I won't stop praying for your salvation, Deanna, but I will stop preaching at you, for now. We miss you back home. There are plenty who'd be happy to see you visit."

She picked at an invisible piece of lint on the side of her leg. "My life is here now. Home is just too. . . ," she let the words die between them.

Randolph stood up, shoving his hands in his pockets. He glanced around the room again. "I'd better go to the hotel," he announced. "I have an early day tomorrow."

She felt a surprising sting of disappointment. "Will you be in town long?" she asked.

"Just long enough," he said. "Perhaps we can get together some more before I leave."

Did she really want that? "I know you're busy," she said, but what she really meant was leave me alone.

Her father, ever intuitive, folded his hands over the back of the kitchen chair. "It brings me pleasure to see you, Bud, even though I worry about you."

Before she could respond, he moved around the table, leaned over, and kissed the top of her head. Without saying another word, he walked out of the duplex. Dee sat glued in her chair, listening intently to the sound of his heavy steps as he headed down the stairs, crunched along the drive, opened and closed his car door. The engine made a high-pitched whine as it roared to life. Her father idled it there for several minutes. She could imagine his head bowed in prayer, parked out there on the street. Finally, she waited until the only sound around her house was that of the cicadas playing their sad, lonely song just outside the window. She sat that way a long time, until the sun rose and the only sounds came from the melancholy chirping of the squirrels barking between the trees just beyond the neighbor's fence.

Her father's words kept going round and round in her mind. She understood what he meant. By choosing to be dead to Jesus, Dee had also chosen to live with the burden of sin, a living death. Could Jesus really forgive any sin, even one as terrible as her own?

Chapter Seven

Brother Thomas bounced the basketball slowly, rhythmically back and forth between each hand, his eyes following Tank, who stooped over the furnace, trying to make the old machine run again so Brother Thomas could avoid calling someone for expensive repairs. He made a sort of humming sound that only God could hear as music. Tank sat back on his heels, wiping the sweat from his forehead.

"I never worked this hard in the Army," Tank joked.

Brother Thomas chuckled. "A little sweat never hurt anybody. Aren't you finished yet?"

Tank yanked his head away from the depths of the furnace. "What's your hurry?"

Brother Thomas grinned even wider. "I figure you have another date with that girl of yours, and I need you to check the toilet upstairs before you go."

Tank shoved his head back in the furnace, grazing his head. He grimaced. "No date, sir, no need to hurry," he admitted.

He half expected this news to trigger a major examination, but Brother Thomas surprised him as usual. "Well then, I reckon I can keep you busy all night long."

After finally getting the furnace to work, Tank tackled the toilet. When he came back down, he found Thomas sitting at the table in the little kitchen at the back of the rec center, two steaming cups sitting there, waiting.

Tank took a seat, fighting the urge to just stand there, defiant like the 13-year-old rebel he once was. The steaming cup smelled deliciously of cocoa and marshmallow. He blew across the liquid before taking a tentative sip, his mind busy with thoughts about the EMT training he'd begun the week before, the lessons he wanted to teach the boys in the coming weeks, the light bulbs he kept forgetting to get for the kitchen light at his one-bedroom apartment.

But mostly, his mind fixated on the one thing he kept trying to forget: Dee sleeping on her back porch, Dee looking up at him with that twinkle in her emerald eyes, the sadness in her gaze, always just beneath the surface, hiding her pain. After their last date, Tank felt certain her pain had something to do with her father. If they had anything in common, it might be that.

"If I haven't said so before, I'm glad to have you back," Thomas' voice broke into the silence.

Tank wrapped his long fingers around the warm mug, taking a deep breath. "Figure I owe you a lot more than a few odd jobs here and there." He took another sip of the hot chocolate.

Thomas looked at him. "I don't expect anything from you, you know," he said. "Relationships don't have to be transactional."

"I've never known them to be anything else," Tank muttered.

"Then I feel sorry for you." Thomas pushed the mug away from himself, scraping it along the table. "I can understand your feeling let down by other people. If you've never experienced the least transactional relationship of all, you would have a hard time believing that people can love without expecting anything in return."

"Jesus expects me to submit to Him. That sounds like a transaction to me," Tank said, feeling like a petulant child.

"He who was there when the world was formed, became human, died without sin, nailed to the cross like a criminal, and you think accepting His grace, submitting to His will, a will which has only your ultimate good at heart, is an exchange that could be considered a transaction?"

Now, Tank really did feel like a petulant child. "Well, when you put it that way," he shrugged.

"For my sin, for your sin, Jesus allowed Himself to experience the punishment of hell, a place where God gives us just what we deserve, an existence without Him, all so that we might be saved from that just punishment. We get to experience heaven because Jesus loved us enough to die for us. When we submit to Christ, we're doing that for us, not for Him."

Tank could feel something fluttering in his chest. He rubbed his sternum, distracted. Was Jesus really willing to forgive someone like him? Could he submit to Christ and feel free of the weight of his mistakes, just like that?

Suddenly, Thomas was there, his beefy hand on Tank's shoulder, warm and comforting. "All it takes to begin is a few words, Tucker. You have the rest of your life then, many years to come, to grow in Christ and discover all the advantages of walking with our Saviour."

Tank swallowed, hard. He'd rarely thought about God in his 20 years in the Army. Now, the idea of releasing all the mistakes in his life, letting them just go, appealed. Suddenly, he wanted it more than anything.

He turned and looked at Thomas, determined. "Give me the

words," he said.

∞ ∞ ∞

Dee hummed as she cleaned her breakfast dishes, her mind filled with images of Tank. They'd been dating for weeks now, seeing movies, taking walks in the park, eating out. She found that she could talk very easily to him, more than she had ever confided in someone since before her mother and brother died. She might even be falling in love with him.

But could he love her knowing who she really was, what she had done to her family? She could keep it a secret from him, but that sat like a heavy ball in her stomach. Then again, if she told Tank everything, how could he want to be with her again?

She felt Smokey rub against her ankles, his purr vibrating against her skin, pulling her out of her musings. "Don't worry," she told him, "Your breakfast is next."

As if he understood, the big, gray cat walked over to the cabinet where Dee kept his food and sat, curling his tail around his body and looking at her with the disdain she'd come to love. His tail tapped slowly against the linoleum as he opened his mouth wide, yawning.

Dee had just finished putting his dish in front of him when her doorbell rang. She hesitated to answer it, thinking her father may have come to visit her again. She wasn't up to another round of arguing about God. A knock split the air, hard enough to shake the doorframe. She grinned, more assured that she knew who had come to see her.

Tank stood on her front porch, a box of donuts in his hands. He grinned, causing a warmth to diffuse through her body.

"Morning, darlin'," he said, stepping into the house after Dee pulled open the door. "Thought you might like to start the day with something sweet."

She'd already had a bowl of cereal, but she saw no reason to disappoint him. "Coffee's in the pot," she said, gesturing toward the kitchen.

He sauntered ahead of her with that confident swagger she admired so much. "Got myself a couple of bear claws, but I think you're more of a sprinkles kind of girl."

She laughed. "I told you I have a big appetite. I've even been known to eat a kolache or three."

Tank slid the box onto the table. His eyes skidded to the tea towel she had folded on the counter next to the sink and the bowl and spoon drying on top of it, then back in her direction. "I see you've already had breakfast," he said, cocking his eyebrow at her.

"Very observant of you," she said, reaching for a donut. "Thank you for these. I'm happy to see you."

"Glad to hear it," he said, pouring himself a cup of coffee and straddling one of her kitchen chairs. He picked up a bear claw and took an enormous bite. Once he'd swallowed, he gave her another one of those grins that made her knees weak. "You sure look pretty in the morning light," he told her.

Dee felt the blush climb up her neck, making her face hot. She tucked a curl behind her ear and moved her fingers to the base of her neck. "I planned on going to the pumpkin patch this afternoon," she told him. "Would you like to come with me?"

"A pumpkin patch? Like Charlie Brown? Whatever is there to

do in a pumpkin patch?"

"Hayrides and mazes and time in the great outdoors, to name a few," Dee said, a little defensively.

Tank raised his hands in mock surrender, "All right, you've convinced me," he said, leaning forward with his arms resting on the back of the chair.

Dee studied him. Tank's shoulders looked strong but relaxed, rising and falling with his steady breaths. His face, usually guarded, looked smooth, open. "You seem a little different, today. More relaxed," she said.

He moved his shoulders. "I feel more relaxed," he said, sounding surprised at the fact.

"What changed?"

"I'm enjoying my training," he said, clearing his throat, "and I'm getting baptized tomorrow."

Dee's back stiffened, and she felt as if someone had reached inside her chest and begun to rummage around in the ruins of it. Tank's lightness (there was no other word for it) added to her mixed emotions. Tank cleared his throat again, causing Dee to start.

"Sorry," she said, shaking her head. "My mind just went," she moved her hand in a sweeping motion over her head, "phew." She blew a raspberry and shrugged.

Tank chuckled. "Yeah, I'm kind of the last guy you'd expect to hear say those words, but it's the best decision I've made in this life, darlin'. I haven't quite forgiven myself, but for the first time ever, I feel like I can find a way to forgiving."

"I killed my mother and brother," Dee blurted, the words tumbling out of her mouth. She watched their effect on Tank in horror as the meaning settled in. She hurried to explain herself. "I was driving the car when we had the accident. That's why I don't live in my hometown anymore. It's why I feel uncomfortable around my father."

To his credit, Tank didn't try to excuse her actions. Instead, he reached out and grabbed one of her hands. His fingers engulfed her cold palm, sending warmth up her arm. "I wish that wasn't a burden you carried." He moved his thumb back and forth across her skin.

A silence descended, so that Dee could hear her ragged breaths going in and out. Her body drew in on itself until even her toes curled in her ballerina flats. Suddenly, Smokey jumped up on the table, sliding to a halt in-between them, his tail straight as an arrow as it pointed at the ceiling. Dee used her free hand to slide along his slick fur.

"Your father is a preacher, right?" Tank asked. He continued without waiting for an answer, "I guess I'm wondering why you would turn away from Jesus when you needed Him most."

"I hated myself so much, I didn't think Jesus could care for me anymore," Dee said, grimacing. "And the more my father talked to me about God, the farther away from God I withdrew."

"You know that game where you pair up and fall back into someone else's arms, the trust game? Well, believing in Jesus as my Savior, it feels like that. I'm in freefall, but I know I'm going to land in loving arms."

Dee felt something in her chest heave sideways, like a doorway cracking open and letting in the light. "I can't make up for what I did," she said. "I've been trying to since the accident, but nothing is enough. I know salvation is a gift, not something to be earned, but I can't seem to let go of the feeling that I need to earn forgiveness."

Tank sat back, withdrawing his hand from hers, leaving her cold, uncertain. "So, how's that working for you?" he asked, crossing his arms over his chest.

Dee felt the question like a slap across the face. She blinked a few times, thinking, then realizing with a start that Tank was right, holding a grudge against God had definitely not been working for her. If she made the choice to admit her failures, her utter humanness, to Jesus, wouldn't she finally free herself of the misery that always sat just below the surface?

"I've wasted a lot of years trying to carry my burdens all by myself," she told Tank. "I can't imagine what it would be like to have a clean slate."

"Don't imagine it. Do it," Tank urged.

Dee swallowed. "Will you help me?" she asked the table.

She felt Tank's strong finger lift her chin. Looking into his eyes, she saw the truth of Jesus' words, My burden is light.

"I'll always be here to help you, Dee," Tank promised. "That is, if you'll let me."

They prayed together then, and Dee submitted herself to Jesus' saving grace, repenting of her stubbornness, utterly aware of her unworthiness, feeling her shoulders lighten with each new breath. In the years that followed, she remembered Tank's imagery whenever they faced trying times, knowing she was freefalling into God's loving arms, understanding at last how much of a difference faith made in a life.

No Second Chances

A Novella

*For Christ also suffered once for sins, the righteous for
the unrighteous, that he might bring us to God, being put
to death in the flesh but made alive in the spirit,*
1 PETER 3:18 (ESV)

When Sandra meets Teddy, little does she realize that her relationship with him will lead her to an even more important relationship, her lifetime commitment to Jesus Christ. So, when Teddy asks Sandra to become his wife, she doesn't have any trouble saying yes.

More than two decades after their marriage, Sandra and Teddy have pastored many churches, raised a son who is fully grown and successful in his own right, too busy for visits with his parents. That's all right. As the leaders of their large congregation, they have plenty to keep them occupied. Maybe, that is the problem.

When a young, doe-eyed assistant begins spending more time with Teddy than his wife, little problems through the years rise to the fore. Will Teddy remember his love for Sandra, and more importantly, his commitment to God?

Now

The sun slashed through the kitchen window, turning the diced yellow onion translucent. Her long fingers wrapped around her coffee cup as she raised it to take a sip, the bitter brew mixing with her tears. Onion always had this effect on her, at least so she told herself as she grabbed another from the basket by the sink and began slicing.

A tap sounded against the doorframe behind her. She turned to see Irma Gates, one of the deacon's wives, holding a box filled with her delicious pies. "I thought I'd find you in here," the older woman said as she moved to the long table in the middle of the kitchen where they usually laid out the buffet.

"I needed to keep busy," she said, making a long slice with her knife. "It's been a long time since I got to help out in the kitchen."

Irma walked up to her, laying a hand riddled with liver spots on her shoulder. "But you have so much to do. No one expects you to have time for this."

Sandra Pike laid down her knife, leaning into the counter with her palms spread on each side of the cutting board in front of her. "I miss times like this," she said, "not the reason for preparing all this food, but the coming together of the women of this church to support our families. I miss the stories about your grandchildren and cruises and frustrations with your husbands. It's different now, in so many ways."

She grabbed the knife and another onion to keep her mouth from spilling more of her misery, or, worse still, her suspicions about Teddy and that woman. Sandra closed her eyes tightly and sniffled, counting silently to ten, then twenty. When she opened her eyes again, Irma touched her hand, the older woman's grip surprisingly strong.

"My girl, there isn't a trouble in this world that isn't amplified by that pulpit when your husband is the man preaching from it," she told her, Irma's violet eyes probing into Sandra's with kindness, not judgment.

She felt tempted to spill all her worries then, almost. Instead, Sandra licked her suddenly dry lips and put a bright smile on her face. "Teddy flies in tonight. He's been gone two weeks this time. I guess I'm just feeling more sentimental than usual."

"Of course you are, dear," Irma agreed, patting Sandra's hand. She glanced around the large kitchen with a practiced eye. "Riser Brown was a popular fellow. I suspect we'll need all those onions. There's nothing like a cheesy casserole to bring some comfort in times of sorrow."

"We better get busy, then," Sandra said, and as if her words had summoned them, the group of volunteers for the funeral committee came into the kitchen, chattering excitedly. The real work began then. If it was the cooking or her own will that brought on her smile, she didn't know for sure.

Much later, she made her way through the cavernous building to her modest office on the second floor. She could remember when her duties as a minister's wife all were handled from the little bureau crammed in the corner of the living room in their tiny duplex. Opening the door to her office, she saw the bureau standing in the corner now, the cheap wood covered in an antiqued white, distressed to give it a shabby chic look, completely opposed to the modern lines of the simple glass desk and office chairs that graced the rest of the room. She sat, giving herself a moment to re-group before beginning the day's next task, answering emails and writing personal notes to various members of the congregation. In just two weeks' time, her biggest event of the year, the Women's Conference, began, and she still had schedules to finalize.

"I knew I'd find you here," a voice said hours later, causing Sandra's heart to stutter in her chest.

Theodore "Teddy" Pike leaned against the doorframe in his three-piece, fancy suit, one hand in his pocket as he smiled at her, revealing his dimples and looking years younger than 48.

"Is it six already?" she asked, finally finding her voice. "You look like you had a good trip."

"It would have been better if you'd come along with us," he said, moving into the room but not coming close enough to kiss her hello or even touch her hand.

"I'm sure you and Kate had it well in hand," she said, stumbling over the name. Ever since the young, enthusiastic administrative assistant had begun working for them, they'd grown further and further apart.

That wasn't completely accurate, though. As Teddy's ministry expanded, then exploded like a super nova, he became more preoccupied with material things, like that expensive suit he wore, and had less and less time for her and Danny, their now-grown son.

"You look tired. Maybe we should have dinner out tonight," he offered. Not that long ago, he would have added a *dear* or *darling*.

"There's some casserole in the refrigerator downstairs. Irma insisted she set it aside for us."

He placed his hands on his hips, pushing aside the blazer and showing off his toned abdomen, another new thing. Sandra sucked in her gut, even as her heart continued its stutter. After almost 25 years of marriage, how many women could say they still loved their husbands as much as when they first married? She realized with a start there was a difference between loving and liking. This man standing in front of her seemed more like the Theodore Pike III his father had always dreamed him becoming, not the Teddy Pike who liked sausage pizza and *Star Wars* marathons sitting on the cheap, shag carpet of their tiny, first apartment.

"Hello," he said, waving his hand in front of her face. "I've been talking for five minutes, and you haven't heard a word. Where did you go?"

She shook her head and stood, straightening her skirt nervously as she rose. "Sorry, just conference stuff. I'm not sure I'm going to finish it all in time."

Usually, people in Kate's position would be responsible for helping Sandra with the big event, but Teddy had insisted he needed plenty enough from Kate to keep her busy full time. At least he had the good grace to blush. "I should be able to get a few of our good ladies to come in extra to help you."

"I can get my own help," she snapped.

The vein in his jaw twitched as he bit down, grinding his teeth. "If you don't want to go someplace nice to eat, we'll just take the casserole home."

She wanted to snap some more, ask him if he intended to stay home all night or fly off for some emergency and be gone into the wee hours. Instead, she forced a half-smile. "A casserole at home sounds wonderful."

They walked out of the mega church to the parking slots nearest the huge complex of buildings, separating at the twin Mercedes XLs Teddy had insisted they buy. She felt like an imposter every time she sat behind the wheel. She watched him walk away from her and get into his car. Still, he hadn't given her so much as a pat on the shoulder, much less a kiss.

Time to face facts, she told herself as she started the car, feeling the powerful engine vibrate her very being. This man who had loved her, encouraged her, nurtured her for more than two decades didn't see anything that he loved anymore. She flipped down her visor, looking in the mirror. Fine lines had begun around her brown eyes, and she had more padding on her face and body than when she was 18 and first met and fell in awe of Teddy Pike, then college senior.

Teddy had changed, too. He looked 30 again with his toned body and new clothes. He'd started using an expensive stylist for his thick hair instead of letting her cut it in the kitchen while they discussed his day and hers. His sermons had changed, too, gaining a more secular flair that sometimes bordered on telling people what they wanted to hear rather than God's truth.

Sandra had to do something. She wasn't just about to fight for her marriage. She had to fight for Teddy's very soul.

Then

Sandra closed her College Algebra textbook, rubbing the back of her neck. She looked up from her library cubicle for the first time in hours, surprised to notice through the distant windows that the sun had set. Sure enough, the squeak of a speaker sounded from overhead, followed by the announcement that the library would close in ten minutes.

She gathered up her study things, shoving them into her backpack. Her stomach grumbled, reminding her she'd last eaten hours ago and then only an apple and a spoonful of peanut butter. Making her way to the elevators, she opted for the stairs, pushing the heavy door forward and letting it swing shut behind her, clanging in the tall, empty space.

The stairwell had just enough light not to trip over herself and a dank, old smell that made her think of the rustic cabin where her family used to vacation years ago, back when Daddy told them ghost stories as they sat all huddled around the potbelly stove, those wonder years before he left them, disappearing for good.

Laughing at her memories to shake the sudden shaft of fear and sadness running through her, she grabbed the slick handrail and started down the stairs at a little bit of a run. She flew down one flight of stairs, then another, her red sneakers a streak of color in the gloom. By the fourth level, she came to a plop on the landing, taking a moment to catch her breath.

"Did Mrs. Bowery catch you with a reference book outside the reference section?" a deep, male voice asked her, causing her to jump slightly as she grabbed fast to the handrail.

She turned to see *him,* the fit, red head who came to the little coffee shop where she worked and ordered the same thing almost every day at 8 am, a large house brew, black. He paid with cash and often placed his change in the TIPS jar on the counter. She had been working up the courage to say more than *hello* to him for weeks now.

Realizing with a start that he stood waiting for an answer from her, she forced a smile to her lips. He smiled back, giving his face a wonderful glow. "I was wondering what had you moving in such a hurry," he explained, his voice smooth, encouraging.

"Truthfully, I spooked myself out a little bit. I didn't realize the stairwell was so creepy."

He moved away from her. "I'll walk the rest of the way with you, if that will make you feel better. I'm Teddy, by the way."

"Nice to meet you, Teddy," she said, trying to push down the stab of disappointment that he hadn't recognized her from the coffee shop. "I'm Sandra." She started down the stairs again, at a much slower pace this time.

"You really should have a buddy to run around campus this time of night," Teddy told her, making her feel like a ten-year-old instead of practically an adult.

"I'm a freshman," she said. "I haven't had much chance to make friends." She had always struggled to get close to people, especially since Daddy left them when she was 14. Neither she nor Mama had been the same since.

"I'm a part of a Christian group. We meet at Boyer Hall at least a couple of times a week. You're welcome to join us," Teddy offered.

"I'm not very religious," Sandra hedged, her fingers flexing involuntarily.

"That's okay," he assured her. "We won't brainwash you or

anything."

"That's not what I meant." She bit on her lower lip, feeling foolish.

They'd reached the bottom of the stairs. He pushed open the heavy door and held it open for her. "Well, I hope you'll think about it. I'd like to see you some time besides just at the coffee shop." He reached inside the outside pocket of his backpack, pulling out a piece of paper and jotting something down. "Here are the dates and times. If you're interested."

She felt too stunned to manage an answer. He did remember her from the coffee shop. Before she could regain her composure, he gave her another dazzling smile. "My girlfriend works at the circulation desk. Can we take you somewhere?"

Deflated, Sandra shook her head. "I'm good. Thank you."

Before he could say something more, she hurried out of the library, into the evening air, which felt brisk, cooling her heated cheeks. Of course, someone as handsome as Teddy would have a girlfriend. Sandra took a moment to imagine how tall and pretty the other woman must be, then she forced her mind onto other subjects.

Reaching her dorm, she felt the music blaring from her room before she even heard it. As she reached the door, she smiled at the chalk board her roommate, Lizzie, had hung on it. Each day, she changed the message written there. Today's read: *The trouble with having an open mind is that people will insist on coming along and trying to put things in it. --Terry Pratchett.*

She pushed open the door to see Lizzie at her desk, her curly, blond hair bouncing with the rhythm of the music as she tapped her pencil against the open textbook in front of her. Sandra threw her backpack on top of her bed and flopped on it dramatically. Lizzie turned sideways, resting her head in her palm.

"Did you miss dinner in the cafeteria again?" she asked.

Sandra's stomach growled accommodatingly. "No, I mean, yes, I missed dinner. But that's not what has me down. He was at the library, and I was a total idiot."

"He who?"

"Lizzie, you know who. He has a girlfriend."

Lizzie blew a bubble with the gum she perpetually had in her mouth. She popped it, pulling the gum back into submission with her lips. "What's that piece of paper in your hand?"

Sandra looked down at it as if she had forgotten all about it. She waved the paper in the air. "He invited me to this Christian thing. I thought it might be a way to get to know him better, but there's no sense now." She crumpled the paper up and tossed it toward the trash bin in the corner. It hit the edge, bouncing back to the floor.

Lizzie bounced up from the chair, turned down the volume on her radio, and picked up the slip of paper, smoothing it against her bare leg below the shorts she wore. "What kind of Christian group?" she asked, looking up at Sandra. For once, Lizzie's eyes had lost their playful glow. In fact, Sandra thought her friend was holding her breath.

Sandra sat up straight, pushing herself against the wall at the head of her bed. She drew her knees up to her chest and hugged them to her body. "You know, most Christians seem pretty stuffy, always trying to judge you and cram their religion down your throat. But Teddy was really so nice to me, and he said their group wasn't anything like that."

"I've been evaluating religious experiences around the world," Lizzie tilted her head into thinking mode. "A few meetings with this group could probably be a big help." She flopped at the foot of Sandra's bed. "You wouldn't mind coming with me? After all, you were the one he invited."

"I'll do it for you," Sandra agreed. "You just have to promise to keep me away from him, no small talk, no nothing. I'm not even going to dress up for it. I don't want him to think I'm a stalker or something."

"He gave you the time and place of this thing, right here," Lizzie tossed the note on top of Sandra's drawn knees. "Showing up is just taking him up on his invitation, nothing more."

"What do you expect to learn there?"

"I dunno," Lizzie shrugged. "I guess maybe why they think Jesus is all that. No one's ever given me a reasonable answer."

Sandra felt her face go hot. Wasn't there a memory, tucked somewhere in between the pages of those idyllic summers she'd spent at her grandmother's farm, some initiation into the mysteries of belief and faith? She shook the idea out of her mind.

"So, are you coming with me for a burger? Ozzie's is opened for another hour."

Now

Teddy took the long way home, driving past the park with its tall oaks and benches where he and Sandra used to sit and watch the neighborhood children on the playground equipment as they held hands and talked about the this and that which wove the fabric of a strong marriage. Could he remember the last time they'd been there?

The sounds of her shower filled the otherwise still house as he stepped inside the foyer, pausing there with his hands stuffed in his pockets, thinking. His sermon the upcoming Sunday needed something more, an oomph he couldn't quite conjure. Perhaps something from Amos would do the trick, or an example from one of the latest scandals filling social media.

Silence descended as Sandra turned off the water upstairs. Too bad she didn't like going to the gym with him. He'd offered to take her more than one time, even offered to hire her a trainer. He'd started working out because Kate made a comment about men with muffin tops one day, and it had started him thinking.

Kate, with her bouncy curls and brilliant smile, made him think about the daughter they never had. At least, this is what he told himself in the wee hours of the night when he woke up in a heavy sweat. She helped him see a younger perspective, giving his sermons the life they needed to fill the sanctuary. Kate kept his dreams of a true megachurch under his pastorship alive. She had suggested breaking from the Southern Baptist Convention and creating a church as church should truly be, with a modern perspective to reach the people who really needed reached.

Sandra called to him from the kitchen, drawing his attention back to the moment. She looked at him oddly as he just stood there with his hands in his pockets right in front of the door. He blinked twice, seeing his wife as if she belonged on the reel of an old, 1950s-style movie, with her hair pulled back in that bun at the nape of her neck in that old, yellow housecoat she'd had for decades. He'd spent so much time with Kate lately, he had a sudden pang of regret at his life choices. Guilt instantly followed this thought, along with a sense of utter surprise.

What cause did he have to regret marrying Sandra, who kept the women's programs at the church running, eased hurt feelings and squabbles among the deacons' wives, and made their house a home, even in those long-ago days when home was a five-hundred square foot loft above Pastor Reynold's garage?

He felt her warm fingers against his arm and started. He couldn't remember the last time they'd even touched each other.

"Are you all right?" she asked in a soft voice, her standard, lemon verbena fragrance wafting from her, making his nose tickle.

"Just thinking about my sermon this Sunday," he said. Hesitating, he laid his hand over her fingers and squeezed, hearing her quick intake of breath. "We should go to the Grove after, maybe take a picnic," he said on impulse. "The weather is supposed to be lovely."

She seemed to hesitate, but then a brilliant smile broke out, reminding him of the Sandra he'd met in a stairwell a lifetime ago. "I'd like that very much."

They wandered into the kitchen together, a companiable silence descending around them as she took the casserole from the oven and placed some of it on two plates. They ate quietly, quickly, a habit developed from long years of jumping up from dinner tables to answer distress calls.

He finished first, leaving half the serving on the plate. He'd sacrificed many a good meal for his new look, not that Sandra had seemed to notice. She used to turn in their bed and nibble on his ear, but he couldn't remember the last time. He hadn't done more than kiss her lips perfunctorily in months, but somehow that reality slipped right past his notice.

Kate had kissed his cheek before they parted ways at the airport that evening, a quick, bright peck on his skin that sent a quickening to his heart. The thought of it fueled another wave of guilt. He pushed it back with effort.

"You won't believe the number of calories a simple casserole can contain," he said, an innocent comment, even though part of him knew it would upset her. At least an argument would cover up the guilt gnawing at the edge of his conscience.

Her shoulders slumped, and a familiar tightness pulled at the corners of her mouth. The look reminded him of those times when he would watch her in the coffee shop, trying to make the foam on the cappuccinos look just right. He'd seen the same look whenever she'd falter over their son's homework she was checking or over the recipe for four she was trying to stretch for forty.

"There's some leftover cobbler in the refrigerator," she said instead of taking up an argument with him.

"I'll pass. I'll be in the study."

She cut off his sentence, "working on Sunday's tricky sermon." She got up from the table, taking both of their plates to the sink. She turned on the water, studying the porcelain. "I used to help you with those," she said into the quiet.

Well, he wasn't the only one thinking about the past lately. An image came to his mind of one wintry afternoon that began with them behind his desk studying the book of 1 Corinthians and ended with them wrapped up in a blanket in front of the fireplace. The feelings welled in his chest, so that he had to rub his sternum to work out the kinks.

"There's some Pepto in the medicine cabinet," she said, pulling him back to the moment. She looked lost. He could see the hurt and the heat in her eyes, veiled by a forced calmness.

He got up from the table and walked over to her, wrapping his arms around her from behind, drawing her to him with his hands resting under her ample breasts. He nuzzled her ear and kissed her neck, but the actions seemed stilted. She felt it too, pulling away his hands and stepping sideways, out of his grasp.

"You have a sermon to finish," she said, her voice a little breathless.

"Sandra," he stopped himself. He'd almost confronted her. But then, he hadn't really meant to seduce her. He hadn't thought about himself or Sandra in that way for a long time, probably since the boy finished college and started working at that investment firm.

She turned to look at him. When he didn't say anything, she wrapped her arms around her middle and let out a sharp breath. For a moment, he thought she might ask the question that seemed to hang around them like a bad smell. Instead, she licked her lips and exhaled a long breath.

"I'll be in the study," he finally said, turning away from her. By the time he reached his desk, all thoughts about his marriage dissipated as he turned his mind back to the text for his Sunday services.

Why hadn't she asked him? Instead, she'd excused him to his sermon, leaving herself feeling vacant.

Another thought came to her mind. Why hadn't she given

in to him and the moment? Looking down at her faded, yellow robe, she knew why. She didn't even like looking at herself in the mirror without her shapewear. She needed to make time for some exercise, eat more leafy greens. Except she knew that would lead to a moment of facing the truth. Even if she had the body he met her in, she doubted Teddy still found her attractive.

The phone rang, making her jump. She hurried to answer it. Crisis followed, as often happened in a minister's household. She spent the rest of the night dealing with one thing and then another until she fell into bed after midnight. She barely noted the bed was empty before succumbing to a fitful sleep.

The next morning, her alarm trilled at 6 am, jarring her awake. She turned her head to the side to see Teddy's empty pillow. She'd find his dirty spoon in the sink, just a hint of leftover yogurt stuck to the sides. She sat up, feeling the emptiness of the house as it closed in around her. The feeling had grown since Danny had landed his dream job, halfway across the country.

She pulled her legs into a crisscross position and bowed her head, praying for her son, her upcoming conference, the Adams' boy who needed surgery, and a host of other concerns about different members of the congregation. She left Teddy to last, as always, asking for strength in his ministry and for his health. She prayed for him to love her again, too, though she felt a sense of despair clawing at the edge of her words.

As she finished making the bed, Teddy walked into the bedroom, surprising her in more ways than one with his lounge pants and nothing more, exposing the hard-won results of his almost daily workouts at the gym. Sandra's heart did a flip-flop in her chest. She felt her lips go dry and licked them before she could say a word. For one crazy moment, she thought about abandoning her reservations and making her move on him, but pride held her back.

"I thought you were gone already," she said then, stumbling over the words.

He quirked an eyebrow at her. "Planning on something you don't want me to see?"

One time shortly after they'd married, he'd come back for some papers after heading out to work to find her sitting on the bed gorging on a Boston cream pie. They'd laughed about it for years after. She hadn't thought about it in a coon's age. Did he remember it?

Still feeling self-conscious about her added weight, Sandra decided not to explore the topic. "Of course not. I just figured you'd already be at the gym."

"Kate had an appointment this morning," he said, nonchalant.

"Maybe I should start coming with you to the gym," she blurted, hating the sting of his words. She felt her pride again and added, "You know, if you need a woman with you to work out."

Teddy stopped in the middle of pulling a shirt from his closet. "That's not fair," he said in that low voice of his, the one he used on Danny when he misbehaved. "I asked you to come to the gym before."

"Yes, well, who has the time?"

"You make time for the things that are important to you," he said, buttoning his shirt with jerky movements.

Sandra sat down hard on the bed. "Yes, you do," she agreed, softly.

He stepped in front of her, forming the knot on his tie as he spoke, "You don't seem yourself lately. Maybe after the convention, you should take a little holiday."

He hadn't said they should take a holiday, only herself. Sandra swallowed the lump in her throat. "Perhaps," she managed.

Leaning down suddenly, he pecked the top of her head. "Think about it. I'm off to work."

Sandra watched him leave the room, listened to him bound down the stairs, heard the front door open and close again. She sat listening to the sounds of the house for a long time after: the drip of the faucet in the guest bath down the hall, the creak of the windows as the wind blew outside, bashing the branches of the fruitless mulberry against the glass, the grandfather clock ticking from downstairs.

She listened until her heart quit beating triple time in her chest, until she could slough off the feeling that her marriage, once vibrant and warm, lay bleeding and cold in a heap before her.

At least this time she didn't shed a tear.

Then

Lizzie stood outside Boyer Hall, tapping her foot in frustration, as Sandra came running up to her, breathless.

"I almost went in without you," she chastised.

They had attended several of the Christian group's meetings so far, but Sandra couldn't stand the idea of drawing any attention to herself, especially by walking into the meeting alone. Teddy's girlfriend looked like a model. Tall, sleek and blonde, she drew the attention of all in any room. Watching Teddy sit beside her during meetings gave Sandra a sweet sort of pain. She only continued to come because the meetings gave her something more that had nothing to do with Teddy.

"Professor Bronwyn wouldn't stop talking," Sandra apologized.

They opened the doors to the building, stepping into the dense smell of the polish giving the floors their high shine. Sandra's heartbeat slowed as a sense of calm took over the nearer they came to the room where the meetings took place. Up until a few weeks before, God meant a distant idea of something beyond her limited sphere of want and need. Now, He had become more personal, an everyday connection that Sandra felt pulling her toward something more, something essential to her life's purpose.

Teddy and Daisy, his girlfriend, stood outside the door to the meeting, partially blocking the entrance. Their whispered words sounded urgent, almost violent. Suddenly, Daisy threw her hands out in frustration, then turned on her heel and stormed off. In her hurry, she broke Lizzie and Sandra apart.

She whirled to face them. "You want him, you can have him," she spat at Sandra, then continued down the hall.

Sandra felt her face flame with embarrassment. Lizzie grabbed her hand and squeezed. "That had nothing to do with you," she insisted quietly.

Teddy stepped forward, his hands stuffed in his pockets. "I'm sorry about that," he said.

When Sandra just stood there, staring, Lizzie cleared her throat. "Well, no sense in dwelling. The meeting is about to begin."

Lizzie's words seemed to break Teddy from his stupor. He shook himself slightly as if to free the thoughts holding him in place. "Yes, it is. Ladies first." He stepped back and gestured them forward.

Sandra settled into her chair in a daze. Lizzie leaned toward her so that she could whisper in her ear. "They'll get back together in a fortnight. Don't get your hopes up," she warned.

She wanted to deny Lizzie's prediction, but what was the use? "You're right," she agreed, reaching into her backpack and pulling out the thick, leather-bound book she had purchased shortly after she and Lizzie began attending these meetings. With her finger, she etched the letters in the title, *Holy Bible,* feeling an odd sort of comfort from it.

"Welcome to you all," Teddy said, sounding exactly like himself, not like a man who had just been dumped in front of everyone. "We're going to study from *Matthew* today, the Parable of the Wedding Banquet, Chapter 22."

Sandra forced her mind to concentrate on the moment at hand, as the students read and then discussed the story about the king whose invited wedding guests refused to come. He then sent his servants to find them. The original guests refused, some tormenting and even killing the king's servants. The king then told his servants to go out on the streets and invite as many people as they found to the feast. The king's hall became filled with people of all kinds, good and bad. When the king came to the feast, he saw a person not dressed in wedding clothes. This person, the king had bound and thrown out on the street, where there would be "weeping and gnashing of teeth."

She found the parable both comforting and scary. Sandra, who knew she had no lineage in the kingdom of God, felt reassured to know that He offered salvation to everyone, even someone like her. But knowing that living a Godly life required more than mere belief, but follow-through on that belief, she wondered if she were up to the task. Would God approve of how Sandra conducted herself? How would she know if He approved of her?

As if he could read her mind, Teddy told the group. "Jesus is the only way to salvation. When He says in the story that many are invited but few chosen, He means that even though He offers salvation to anyone willing to believe in and follow Him, few of us choose to do that. But Jesus also tells us that His burden is light. When we bow down in obedience to Him, He helps us do what is right. Belief in Jesus as Savior is the wedding garment we all want to be wearing when the time comes to meet our Maker."

Sandra could feel her heart beating in her chest, as she chewed her lip, thinking about how different her world had come to look in the last few weeks. She hadn't gotten as nervous about her tests as usual, and she'd found it easier to talk to people she didn't know. She knew it all had something to do with her growing faith in a God who loved her, despite all her flaws.

They left the meeting as soon as it had finished, Sandra wanting desperately to keep the holy journey she had begun separate from any feelings she might have for Teddy Pike. How she knew that a separation was vital to her spiritual health, she couldn't explain, not even to herself. Maybe it was part of Jesus putting her in the right wedding clothes.

"What are you smiling about?" Lizzie asked as they came upon their dorm. Her voice sounded serious, as if she knew Sandra's thoughts before she asked for them.

"I was thinking about the parable," she said, "and how I want to be a follower of Jesus."

Lizzie nodded solemnly. She smacked her ever-present gum. "I want that, too."

They stopped in the middle of the sidewalk, causing a few of their fellow students to grumble as they stumble-stepped around them. Lizzie studied her a moment before nudging her in the shoulder.

"What if Teddy really is without a girlfriend? What will you do then?"

Sandra blushed. "Hope for the best?" she asked.

Lizzie looped her arm with Sandra's. "Oh, no," she said, "we can come up with something much more interesting than that to do."

∞∞∞

Teddy opened the door to his dorm room, expecting it to be empty. Instead, his roommate Glen lay sprawled on his bed, his eyes studying the ceiling. Teddy closed the door and moved to the desk on his side of the room, laying his books there, hoping for quiet and time to think.

"So, Daisy couldn't bring you up to scratch," Glen said, bursting in on his thoughts.

"That's not what happened," Teddy said, distractedly. He shuffled the books on the desk, then pulled out the chair with a jerk, plopping into the seat. "I have work to do," he warned Glen.

"I'd say," Glen agreed, sitting up against the headboard. He studied Teddy as he'd studied the ceiling, with a casual interest that belied his words. "It's going to take some work to get a girl like Daisy back."

Teddy turned in the chair to look at his roommate. "How did you even know? It only just happened before Bible meeting. Why were you missing, by the way?"

The question diverted him. "I don't know if I want to continue Biblical studies, Teddy. I'm thinking about something a little more lucrative."

"Why?" Teddy demanded in surprise.

Glen placed his hand on his stomach. "I like to eat," he grinned. Tall and lanky, Glen looked like a strong wind might blow him over. His face turned serious. "I don't like the thought of guiding other people's souls, Teddy."

"And why not, when it's the most righteous occupation in the world?" Teddy stood and moved to his bed so that he could face Glen when he sat. "Didn't God call you to minister?"

Glen started, and Teddy realized he had snapped out the question with every fiber of his being, which currently felt coiled and ready to spring. Teddy took a deep breath and tried to relax, but his muscles refused to cooperate. "I'm sorry, Glen," he said after a moment. "I didn't mean to snap at you."

"It's all right," Glen assured him. He flexed and released his fingers several times. "It doesn't mean I'm throwing away my faith," he insisted.

Teddy breathed in and out again. "No, it doesn't," he agreed. "Still, He puts us here for a purpose. Will you find peace if you aren't fulfilling yours?"

Two beats of silence passed between them, then four. "Are you asking me," Glen said in a quiet, toneless voice, "or yourself?"

Teddy felt the words like a blow. How did Glen know about the doubts that plagued him in the middle of the night? "What will you study instead?" he asked, ignoring Glen's question.

"I don't know," Glen shrugged. "I'm pretty good with figures. Maybe I'll be an accountant."

They sat in silence, looking at each other. Finally, Glen smiled. "Cheer up, buttercup," he teased. "I still believe in God Almighty."

"You had such passion to preach."

"No," Glen stood, as if his energy could not contain itself, and began to pace. "I never felt quite right behind the pulpit, so to speak. There are other ways to serve God without working for a church."

Teddy let that settle in. He'd wanted to be a pastor since he became a teenager. The idea that Glen could want it and then throw the dream away baffled him. It almost made him forget about his other problem.

"Daisy was right to throw me over," he said. "Lately, I've found myself thinking about someone else."

Glen sat back down with his elbows on his knees, leaning forward. "Does this someone else return that interest?"

Teddy swallowed. "I don't know." He shoved his fingers through his hair. "I haven't gotten the courage to speak to her, not more than a few words here and there."

"Really? That is something new. You could speak to POTUS and not hesitate. Who is it?"

Teddy pulled at his collar. "It's the girl from the coffee shop, the one I met in the library."

"But you said she was a freshman, practically a child."

"You should see her face when she thinks no one is looking, especially when we are in a meeting and she learns yet another new thing about Christ. You could light up the room with the glow from her face then."

"So, why don't you take your courage to the sticking place and just talk to her?"

Teddy made a face. "Because she's just beginning to understand what Jesus can mean for her life, and I don't want any possible feelings for me to get in the way of that."

"You think too much," Glen scoffed.

"Maybe," Teddy agreed. He stood up and moved back to his desk, grabbing the nearest book blindly and jerking it open. "You better see the counselor about changing majors if you're really serious. You might even have time yet to switch your classes up." He didn't look at Glen as he said it, just kept his eyes trained on the page in front of him.

Even after Glen left the room a few minutes after, Teddy continued to study pages that he didn't actually see. He believed that Sandra Hill had a good heart, one that could serve God in magnificent ways, but she didn't see that yet. If Teddy put romance in front of God's work, what kind of man would that make him?

Not the kind of man he wanted. He tromped down to the showers and took a long, cold shower, hoping to drown the errant thoughts hounding him to focus on his work.

But Sandra Hill, and maybe God, too, had other plans.

Now

Teddy tapped his expensive Monte Blanc against the table's edge as he listened to Mike Bradley, one of the church deacons, wend and wind his way to his point. Losing patience at last, he blurted. "Where is this going, Mike?"

Bradley stood 6'6" in his stocking feet. He straightened now, seeming even larger. "We promised the missions in Haiti and Laos, as well as our outreach programs here in the states ,that we were going to increase our levels of support by 10% this year. Now, we're hearing there are plans to expand the church itself, that you've had brokers scouring around for acreage sufficient for a significant increase from what we have now."

Teddy raised a hand to stop him. "I see where you're headed with this, Mike. But I'm telling you, this congregation has it in us to provide for our mission commitments and pursue an expansion."

"We've grown this past year, certainly," this from Robert Bryce, who owned a chain of dry-cleaning operations, "but the rate of growth we'd need to achieve these numbers." He stopped, blowing air through his lips.

"I know we can make these numbers work, gentlemen," Teddy insisted, even though he felt his patience growing thin. "With God, all things are possible."

"'But do not forget this one thing, dear friends: With the Lord a day is like a thousand years, and a thousand years are like a day,'" David Clermont, the youngest member of the group said, quoting the Word at Teddy as if he did not live and breathe it every day of his life. "Why not leave all this to God's timing? It seems to me as if we're trying to do the opposite."

Teddy exhaled, laying his pen with slow deliberation upon the table. He rose. Decades of meetings much like this one, being told how to do his job by men who meant well, by a system God Himself may have ordained but men surely muddled, closed in on him suddenly.

"We may not agree on what this congregation can do, gentlemen, but I know what I can lead a congregation to accomplish. I will make this dream happen, with or without the Southern Baptist Convention behind it."

His closest friend among them, Eli Matthews, stood beside him, laying a hand on Teddy's shoulder. "Don't speak hastily, Brother," he entreated. "Much prayer is needed, and no one has actually said no."

"Yet," Teddy ended the sentence for him, sloughing away from his contact. "No one has said no yet." He glanced at his watch impatiently. "I have other meetings. If you'll excuse me."

He slipped out of the room and hurried out of the building to avoid a confrontation he would regret. He grabbed his cell from his pocket and dialed it. He needed to talk to the one person in the world who would understand his frustration.

"Hello," the voice on the other end of the line answered. "Where are you?"

"I need to talk to you, away from the church. Can you get out of the office without being noticed?" he asked.

"No problem. Where do you want to meet?"

He thought a moment. "The gym. You have your workout clothes?"

She chuckled low in her throat. "Always. I'll meet you there in fifteen minutes."

He ended the call, making his way through the large

parking lot to where he'd parked his car that morning. His pulse beat in his neck with the adrenaline pumping through him. He felt as if his whole world were on the verge of a new discovery, something life-changing. And he realized with a start that he wanted *her* to be a part of it.

He had just settled into a quick, six-mile speed on the treadmill when she bounced onto the machine next to him, offering him that brilliant, beautiful smile.

"Now, what's troubling you, Teddy?" Kate purred, making his blood run hot. "Tell little Katy girl all about it."

$\infty\infty\infty$

News of Teddy's outburst and exit reached Sandra's office in record time. Robert Bryce found her sitting behind her desk, staring blankly at the planning pages in front of her. The lean man sat down in one of her guest chairs without even asking permission, crossing his legs.

"Your husband has some big ideas, Sandra," he said.

She tried, and failed, to hide her grimace. "What do you plan on doing about it?"

"I'm hoping you might help us. Is there something troubling Teddy at home?"

She straightened her spine. "What do you mean?"

"He seems on edge. It makes our job more difficult when he gets so agitated that he won't even listen."

Sandra placed her palms on top of the desk and breathed. "Are you trying to get me to do your job for you?" she asked on a laugh, trying to lighten the tension in the air.

Robert uncrossed his legs, laying his elbows on his knees. "I'm trying to determine if your husband needs to take a sabbatical before he draws a line none of us want to cross."

Her heart dropped to her stomach. She wanted to open her mouth and tell Robert Bryce in no uncertain terms that Teddy Pike only wanted to follow where he felt Christ led him, but since she herself had doubted Teddy recently, she couldn't bring herself to say it. Instead, she forced a smile to her lips. "I'm sure everyone will cool off soon enough and come to a reasonable compromise."

Robert stood, shoving his hands in his pockets. "Well, keep the thought in mind. A couple of months away, at my lake house, wouldn't do the two of you any harm. Teddy could work on his next sermon series. And we men all know how hard you women work. You deserve a break, too."

"Thank you, Robert. That's very generous of you."

"You think about it," he said again, nodding once before turning on his heel and leaving her office again.

Sandra waited for the count of ten before jumping to her feet and pacing around the office, brushing her hands down her skirt. If she called Teddy now, she knew he wouldn't answer, and that would break her heart. When was the last time he'd talked to her about any of his decisions? So long ago she couldn't remember when.

Rhonda Ware, the church secretary, stopped in her doorway. "Kate's left early. Again," she said flatly. "Where do you reckon she goes, when she leaves like that?"

"You can go home any time you like, Rhonda," Sandra said with a tight throat.

The older woman raised both hands defensively. "Your point is taken, Sandra. It's none of my business. I just hate to see your good nature taken advantage of."

Sandra grabbed the flyer from her desk. "Could you make sure the printer gets this before five?" she asked, hoping to get rid of the other woman before she said something ugly, or worse yet, burst into tears.

No, she didn't feel like crying, more like hitting something. Rhonda took the flyer with a timid smile and nodded before heading back down the hall. Sandra sat back against her desk, tapping her fingers against the edges. Maybe Robert was right. A sabbatical away from the church for a couple of months would give her a chance too.

Her thoughts ground to a halt, and she stood up, starting to pace again. How did you win back your husband when your competition was younger, prettier, and without the baggage any relationship of twenty-plus years carried? Her papers, splayed on the desk, caught her attention. She had so much work to finish. She forced herself to sit at the desk again.

Two minutes later, she gave up trying to accomplish anything. She couldn't concentrate, and when she did manage to focus, she could only see one thing, and that was Teddy in the arms of another woman. Deciding her thoughts could be so much foolishness, Sandra gathered her purse after shoving her papers into her briefcase. She left the building, heading straight for her car.

Once inside, she finally pulled out her cell and dialed her husband. The phone rang and rang, finally going to voicemail. Sandra opened her mouth, but no sound came out. She heard the other end beep before hitting end on her cell. It was better that way, she decided. He could pretend he didn't see the missed call much easier than ignoring a voicemail from her.

But was she afraid or just indifferent? She recalled with certain clarity that moment twenty years ago when she'd all but forced Teddy to proclaim his love for her if he wanted to keep her. Where was that fire now?

Her cell rang, startling her from her mental ramblings. For an insane moment, she thought it might be her husband. Instead, she saw that it was her son Danny calling. She immediately answered, but before she could say a word, Danny's authoritative voice demanded, "What is this about Dad leaving the church?"

"Don't be ridiculous," she answered. "Who called you, anyway?"

"I have friends in strategic places. Seriously, Mom, what's going on with Dad?"

"I don't know, really. How are you, dear? How's the job? Is there a nice girl at your church you've started dating?"

Danny snorted. "Who has time for socializing? I like my job, Mom. Relationships are just too much work with too little reward."

The sentiment shocked her. "Are you telling me you don't think your father and I have a happy relationship?"

Danny made a noise. She could envision his green eyes cast down as he blushed. "Maybe when you spend time together, which I haven't seen in years. Dad always put the church first, and we both know it."

"I'm sorry, Danny. You didn't ask to be born to this life. But I chose it willingly because I felt God's calling. And I love your father."

Someone else said something to him. "I'm sorry, Mom. I gotta go."

"Hope I hear from you again soon," she blurted before the line clicked, ending the call. She grasped the steering wheel with fingers that shook slightly. She had the feeling that something monumental loomed, and she hadn't felt like that since before Danny came along.

She would go home and pray about it, she decided, knowing Him as the One who never failed.

Then

Sandra sat in the library, trying hard to concentrate on the history book in front of her, instead finding herself thinking about a certain red-headed senior. Three weeks had passed since Daisy broke up with Teddy, and he still hadn't asked her out or even so much as flirted with her. To top it off, he had stopped coming into the coffee shop during her work hours.

"Hey, beautiful," said a male voice at her ear, causing her to jump.

She turned to see Bobby Neals, the big, burly sophomore from her chemistry class who was on a football scholarship. Rumor had it he was destined to be a first-round pick in the NFL draft in the next year or two. He had strong, high cheekbones and a square jaw and long, blond eyelashes around his amber eyes that even the girls envied.

"You startled me," Sandra murmured, for want of a better thing to say. "How are you?"

He pulled a chair from a table near the cubicle where Sandra sat and straddled it backward. She watched his hands hanging over the chair, huge like platters, strong fingers that could probably snap a walnut. She had a fleeting thought about the value of those hands, ones that would help earn Bobby millions in his future.

"I'd be better if you'd agree to go out with me," Bobby said, answering her question.

The offer caught Sandra by surprise. "You want to go out? With me?" she squeaked.

Bobby smiled and cocked his head. He reminded Sandra of Snowball, the St. Bernard her neighbors had back home, more cute than handsome, but comfortable and familiar. As she sat there, stunned at his invitation, Bobby reached across the distance between them and gently stroked Sandra's cheek.

"You're as pretty as a sunrise," he said, then pulled his hand away. "How about a movie tomorrow night?"

Sandra had hoped for Teddy Pike for so long, she hadn't made room in her mind to consider anyone else. A tiny door creaked open inside her brain. She smiled shyly at Bobby. "I'd like that."

One movie became two, and then lunches together three times a week, and then Sandra wearing Bobby's jersey like a true girlfriend. Bobby turned out as sweet and puppy-like as she had expected. He called her cute names like *buttercup* and *sweetie pie* and even on occasion, *my little kumquat*. He kissed with a certain sloppy eagerness that Sandra found endearing because it told her he had as little experience in lovemaking as she did, and they never went beyond kisses.

After a few weeks of their going out together, Sandra garnered the courage to ask Bobby if he'd like to join her for Bible club, as she'd come to call it. He gave her a sort of wistful smile and shook his head slowly.

"I've got practice, darling," he drawled in that slow, steady way of his. "Besides, I'm not into that Jesus stuff. Too many obligations."

It was on the verge of her tongue to try to explain to him that his perception was all wrong, but someone came up to him then, wanting to praise him for the last week's game and offer tips for the future. The next thing Sandra knew, Bobby floated away amidst a stream of freshmen wanting a fleeting moment of his attention.

"What are you going to do with a boyfriend who doesn't believe in Jesus?" Lizzie asked, popping her gum. Today's smelled grape flavored and had already left a tiny, purple ring around her lips.

"Do you think you can be in love with someone and not have that little tingle in your nerve endings every time they touch you?" Sandra asked instead of answering Lizzie's question.

Her roommate pulled her knees up to her chin and rested her head there. "Are you saying that Bobby Neals doesn't make you want to jump in bed with him?"

"Lizzie!"

She managed to look indignant. "That's what you're talking about, isn't it? You've been dating Bobby Neals for almost two months now, and he hasn't tempted you to have sex with him. Maybe he feels like sex should be saved for marriage, just like we do. Maybe he hasn't even tried to tempt you because he respects you."

The thought made Sandra feel even more conflicted. "What I'm trying to say, Lizzie, is that I don't think Bobby could tempt me to have sex with him. I just don't seem to feel that way about him."

Lizzie rolled her neck and popped her knuckles. "Is this about Teddy Pike? It's been weeks since he broke it off with his girlfriend, and he hasn't said anything to you outside of Bible club discussions. Maybe Teddy just isn't into you."

Sandra looked up at the ceiling and sighed, closing her eyes tightly. "How do I know for sure, though?"

"You know," Lizzie insisted. After a long pause in which Sandra said nothing, Lizzie continued. "If you want to know for sure if Teddy likes you, you're just going to have to ask him."

Lizzie's words made perfect sense in the security of their shared dorm room, but in the real world of the college campus, Sandra kept losing her nerve, which meant she kept going out with Bobby hoping to feel that little zing she always felt when Teddy drew near.

It might have continued that way except for the weekend of the seventeenth, an off week for the football team, so that Bobby invited Sandra to a Saturday night party at one of the frat houses on campus. Blaring music tumbled out of the open windows, blending with the pungent stench of cheap beer on the air as they approached the bright-red door of the Pi Kappa Alpha house.

"Hey, mate," a burly giant standing guard slapped Bobby on the back. He spoke in a thick, Australian accent, opening the door, so that Sandra almost couldn't hear him over the din. "Save me one for the road," he invited as he stepped aside to give them entrance.

Bobby stopped Sandra before stepping inside. "My girl needs a wristband, Tanzer."

"Really?" the big man questioned. "She looks all right to me."

Bobby extended his palm, rolling and unrolling his fingers. "Gimme."

As Sandra attached the red band around her wrist, she gave Bobby a questioning look. "It tells them you're not legal to drink," he said into her ear so she could hear him.

She turned her lips against his ear then. "You're not legal either," she pointed out.

Bobby just turned his face to hers and wiggled his eyebrows. "Just one beer, buttercup," he assured her. "I've got a game on Wednesday."

The air inside the crowded party felt too close. Sandra knew she would have to throw away the clothes she wore after this. How else would she rid herself of the smell of alcohol and cigarettes? Holding onto Bobby's arm with a death grip, she struggled to keep up with his almost frenetic pace as he made his rounds, saying hello to his friends on his way to getting that *one beer.*

Almost two hours later, Sandra wondered why she had agreed to this party, especially when Bobby downed not just one alcoholic beverage but upward of six, including a few of a shot variety that looked questionable to her. Bobby's usually steady gait had turned into an unsteady shuffle. She felt the weight of him increase as he pulled her onto the makeshift dance floor where everyone gyrated to the heavy bass of the music blasting from the speakers throughout the room.

Bobby's strong arms felt more like dead weights on top of her shoulders as he swayed clumsily with her. She breathed into her t-shirt to reduce the pungent odor of Bobby's breath. There seemed to be another odor in the frat house, too, one that made her head swim. She should really go home. So far, this party had blown her eardrums, blistered her nostrils, and seriously deflated her opinion of Bobby Neals. Now, if she could only get her feet to follow her thoughts.

"Excuse me," a clipped voice sliced through the blare of the music. And then when Bobby kept swaying with her, with more force, "My turn, Bobby."

On another night, Bobby Neals surely would have balked at this challenge, but obviously the beer had mellowed him. "Take good care of her," he slurred out, giving Sandra a clumsy twirl, landing her right into the other man's arms.

Sandra felt the little hairs on the back of her neck stand at attention. She took a moment to collect herself, staring at the third button on his pullover, before looking up at him. Instead of the kind face she thought to find, Teddy's full lips drew into a thin line. His brown eyes bore into hers, sending a not unpleasant shiver down her spine.

"I never expected to see you here," he barked. She decided to give him the benefit of the doubt. Maybe he raised his voice like that because of the music so loud around them.

She half expected him to take her by the hand and pull her out of the party, but instead his arms tightened around her. "Are you all right?" he asked, his voice mellowing.

Mellow, that was a nice, round sort of word, she thought, a feeling like floating gathering in on her. She felt her knees buckle as Teddy's arms swept down and around just in time to catch her from hitting the floor. He smelled of musky cologne and something more that was all himself. Sandra snuggled into his body as he carried her off the dance floor, down the long hall and out into the cool, clear dark. She took another breath of him and moaned out.

"Are you all right, Sandra?" Teddy repeated, shaking her more forcefully this time.

She rolled her head back on his shoulder so she could look at him. My, but she felt like being silly suddenly. "Why don't you like me, Teddy Pike?" she breathed out.

He stopped his march down the long drive of the frat house and let her slide down his body until her feet hit the gravel, making a sad, little crunching sound. "What were you thinking, coming to a place like this?" he demanded.

The words sobered Sandra faster than a bucket of cold water over her head. She felt a blush of shame flame her cheeks. Her hands went to her waist of their own accord. "What business is it of yours?" she demanded right back, trying to hold on to a little bit of pride.

He crossed his arms in front of his chest. "I guess you're right. It is none of my business. You want to go back inside to your," he paused as if searching for the right word, "boyfriend, don't let me stop you."

"Bobby's a nice guy," Sandra defended, hearing Teddy's disdain in the tone of his voice. "And he likes going out with me," she taunted. She swallowed back a wave of nausea, hoping Teddy wouldn't notice. "What are you doing here?"

He pulled at his collar and cleared his throat. "I may have received a phone call from my roommate."

"A phone call about the party?"

Teddy looked up at the sky before turning back to face her. "About your presence at the party."

"So, you thought you had to rescue me." Sandra began to pace in front of him, deflated. "Just because you lead Bible group doesn't mean you're responsible for everyone who attends."

"But I do feel responsible for you, Sandra," he insisted.

It was on the tip of her tongue to ask him *why* when an incredible idea wiggled its way into her brain. Maybe she had the buzz from the dope-laced air at the party to thank for the courage to ask him again, "Do you like me, Teddy Pike?"

He swallowed. Then, instead of saying something, he kissed her.

Now

Teddy pulled into the garage and turned off his car, taking a moment to sit in the silence before easing himself out of the vehicle and gingerly working his way to the door that led to the house. His hand rested on the knob. He looked at it as if his fingers were not attached to the rest of his body.

As he stood wondering, the door fell open, startling loose his nervous grip on it. Sandra stood in the laundry room in her familiar, polka dot pajama set with fuzzy slippers on her feet. Her hair lay loose and ruffled around her head, as if she'd been tossing and turning in bed. Her eyes flashed at him before she took a deep breath and stepped to the side, giving him room to walk into the house.

He closed the door gingerly behind him, as if Danny still lay in his race car bed upstairs. His eyes traveled to his wristwatch, which told him it was 2 a.m. His eyes closed tight on a wave of nausea and disgust. He chanced another look at his wife. *His wife.* The phrase gave him a start that felt like icicles in his abdomen.

Sandra pressed against the wall, away from him, as he walked past her, but she still managed to smell the flowery and earthy scent that clung to him. He heard her sharp intake of breath when it hit her.

"Teddy?" she managed in a tight whisper, all of her questions summed up in that barely-contained emotion he heard in her voice. It stopped him in his tracks.

"Sandra," he croaked, then horrified himself by stuttering his lips like a guppy, no sound except his raspy breath coming out.

"Oh, Teddy," she said again, drawing out the words, her voice thick with tears.

"It's not what you think," he blurted stupidly.

"Right," she snapped, her back stiffening. She swiped at her tears and managed a militant glare before storming away from him.

A small voice in Teddy's head told him he should follow her. He ignored it, sliding past the kitchen like a scolded dog and making his way up to the guest bedroom. For once not caring about his expensive suit, he pulled his clothing from his body, letting it fall where it may, and crawled under the watermelon comforter covering the full-sized bed, closing his eyes.

Five minutes later, he pushed himself to a sitting position against the headboard, breathing heavily. Whenever he closed his eyes, images raced behind his lids, images that made his palms clammy. He shoved his fingers through his hair and strained to listen to the quiet of the house for signs of Sandra's movements.

Something downstairs crashed, followed by the sound of elephants tromping through a room. Teddy winced at the noises. Nausea rose in his throat, and he struggled to swallow it down. If the deacons could see him now. He let that thought hang in the air and even made a swiping motion with his hand as if to push it away.

Just when he managed to calm his heart beating out of his chest, the door to the guest room banged open and slammed into the wall. The whites of Sandra's eyes gleamed in the semi-dark of the gloomy room. He pushed his forehead into his palms to escape her scrutiny.

"I want to hear you say it," she demanded, her voice toneless.

"It's late. Go to bed," he countered. It took all his willpower not to curl into the fetal position and pull a pillow over his head. Instead, he managed to raise his eyes to hers.

"Is it your megachurch?" she swallowed, "Do you think you need a younger woman to go with it?"

"Don't be stupid," he blurted. He saw the words leave his mouth in slow motion and longed to pull them back.

But instead of exploding at him like he deserved, Sandra pulled into herself. "If you're determined to break God's law, how do I stop you?" she wondered aloud in a small voice, as if she were a child crying to her mother. When he didn't say anything, she asked into the quiet, "Why did you even come home to me?"

He swallowed back the words that sprang to his lips. They tasted bitter and slid down his throat, burning. Just because he wanted something bigger and better. He stopped his thoughts. The megachurch, his dream, had nothing to do with Kate. She supported him, sure, which was more than he could say for Sandra, but wanting something better for his church wasn't what had Sandra shooting daggers at him with those eyes.

The skin on the back of his neck felt like it flamed. "You deserve better, Sandra," he admitted, even though his neck tightened like it might snap with the admission. His next words sounded strangely like a plea. "I don't want to go anywhere," he said.

It would have helped him if she had said something tacky, screamed, thrown something directly at his head. Instead, she let out a whimper before re-gaining control of herself. "I can't stay here anyway," she muttered to herself, the words ominous.

Before he could react, she pulled the door closed softly. He could imagine her leaning her forehead against the wood for a long moment before turning down the hall to head toward their master bedroom. His limbs felt detached from his body as he lay in the bed waiting for something, maybe an answer from God?

It wasn't a good time to be asking God questions. Or Sandra, either. He slid into the mattress, pulling the covers on top of himself.

∞ ∞ ∞

She walked down the hall to her bedroom with the sound of her heartbeats pounding in her ears, her movements careful, stiff. At least the tears had stopped. She yanked at the front of her soaked pajama blouse, pulling it away from her skin. The room felt hot and her body too large for her skin.

A few moments later, she stood naked under the cool spray of the showerhead, washing away the heat but not the tension from her muscles. So many thoughts jumbled through her brain, leaving her feeling exhausted. Perhaps she should crawl into bed.

As tempting as sleep sounded, she knew her mind would race with unwanted thoughts and questions the moment she closed her eyes. Better to pack a bag. She glanced around the room, cavernous, larger than their first three apartments. He'd moved them here last month, surprising her with this seven-thousand square-foot mansion when she had been ready to downsize from the three-bedroom ranch where they'd lived since Danny's last year of high school.

This house was enough for them to get lost in, isolated away from each other. Teddy could certainly come and go without her ever knowing it, especially if she didn't stay up watching like a hawk. She wished she hadn't stayed up this night. No telling how long she might have carried on as if nothing had changed if she had just avoided meeting him as he walked in from the garage earlier.

She'd never seen the Grand Canyon. If she got started in another hour, she could stop in Albuquerque for lunch, maybe visit Old Town. Or maybe she didn't care if she went anywhere except away from *him* for the time being.

She'd always been one to run away from confrontation, only to have him run after her. Any other time, he'd already have arrived in the room beside her, forcing her to talk out their problem together. She stilled, listening, hoping against hope to hear his footstep in the hall.

With renewed vigor, she shoved clothes and toiletries into some luggage and took everything down the stairs, letting the wheels bounce noisily against the steps. In her car, she turned off the radio and drove to the hotel in silence, one on the outskirts of town where no one would know her. No sense giving tongues even more reasons to wag.

Why did she care what others said? She thought about that question as the elevator moved up to the tenth floor. Her life's work had involved supporting her husband as the "perfect" reverend's wife. Could she remember a time when she'd wanted something else, perhaps something more? As she prepared herself woodenly for bed, she flexed her numb fingers, pulling the covers back and crawling in between the crisp sheets. Still, her mind continued to skid through a million unanswered questions.

Morning came before her heavy lids gave way to sleep, obliterating her racing thoughts and allowing her to finally get some much-needed rest. When she woke and looked at the clock, it read 5:42 p.m. She had slept the day away.

Pulling herself up against the headboard, Sandra reached to the side table for her cell, which she had turned off before getting in the bed. Powering it up now, she almost jumped out of her skin when the phone began to ring and vibrate in her hand. It was Danny, which surprised her into answering the call.

"Where are you?" he demanded sharply, though she could hear relief in his voice.

"Just resting," she evaded his question, asking her own, "How are you?"

"How am I?" he repeated, and his voice rose an inch. "I've been calling you since last night." She heard the noise around him abate as the click of a door sounded. In the silence, she could hear his breath, in and out, in and out, before he finally broke the tension with a sigh. "What's going on, Mom?"

"I'm not sure." The admission, slipping past her lips before she could stop herself, surprised her into a hiccup. "Don't worry about me, honey," she added, feeling the sadness bear down on her, the pain of it slicing through her.

"Should I schedule a flight?"

The offer tempted her. A visit from Danny would allow her just the excuse she needed to ignore her crisis and concentrate on spoiling her kid, even if he was a grown man. But that would only delay the inevitable. "No," she managed, though her throat felt too tight, "I don't see any reason for you to disrupt your plans."

"Dad is looking everywhere for you," Danny said, sounding more like himself. "Promise me you're going to call him."

As if they had timed it, her phone began to vibrate as the second call came through.

"Is that him?" Danny asked, then, "I'll hang up so you can answer. Love you, Mom."

Suddenly, the phone began ringing in her ear. She pulled it

back to look at the picture she had connected to Teddy's contact information. She'd taken it at the end of one of their mission trips. They'd travelled to Guadalajara, Mexico, spending the days building a school for junior high girls. Covered in sweat and dirt, Teddy grinned at the camera, showing the crinkles at the side of his eyes and the dimples in his cheeks, reminding her of the husband she'd had in the beginning of their marriage.

Maybe that image, the memory of his kindness, devotion, and attention, made her next decision for her. She took in a deep breath and clicked the green button on the face of her cell. She had to work her mouth several times before she managed a wretched-sounding *hello.*

"Where have you been?" Teddy demanded, causing a flood of heat to her chest.

"What do you care?" she blurted. "I don't think I need to tell you where I have been ever again." She paused, taking a deep breath that rattled in her lungs and shook the bed. "Do you love her?"

A beat of silence sliced the air between them, then two. Finally, Teddy managed a rather weak, "Don't be ridiculous."

She licked her lips. They tasted salty from her tears, with just a hint of the stale coffee she'd picked up at the gas station where she'd stopped before taking off on the road. "You've replaced me with a younger model, and I'm the one being ridiculous? Do you love her, Teddy? You didn't answer me."

"I'm married to you," he said, but something in the way he said it made Sandra feel as if her whole world had crumbled.

"Did you sleep with her?" she demanded, her hands tightening of their own volition, one on the hard case of her phone, the other scrunching the hotel's soft sheets.

"Sandra," he exclaimed, but he didn't answer her question.

Silence, tense and hard, descended between them. Finally, she broke it. "I'm not coming back to that mcmansion you've moved us into. I never should have agreed to it in the first place."

"Think of the church," he cajoled. "We're at a critical time for the new building. Think about the message you'll be sending to our congregation."

"I don't think I'm the one who should think about what kind of messages are being sent to our congregation." She pushed herself off the bed and began to pace around the room. "I can't believe this is happening. I knew you were in trouble, but I never thought you'd go this far."

"I know you're at the Bridgerton Hotel, Sandra, now that you've turned your phone back on. I'm half way there already. We'll talk more when I get there."

Before she could respond, Teddy ended their call together, leaving her standing in the middle of the unfamiliar room, her eyes shimmering with still more tears in them. "It can't have come to this," she panted.

It suddenly became important that she look her best, and she didn't have much time to finish the job. She grabbed her cosmetics bag from her luggage and hurried to the bathroom, hoping she could gather up some of her lost confidence with some magic from ULTA. All those years, all the sacrifices she'd made. An image of Bobby Neals flashed into her brain. He hosted Friday night football on one of the major sports networks these days, now that he was retired from a successful career in the NFL. She might have been a football player's wife instead of a preacher's. At least being cheated on would not have been such a surprise, then.

"God," she prayed, closing her eyes, "take this pain from me. Thy will and not my own."

Minutes like hours ticked by before Teddy knocked rapidly on the hotel room door. She smoothed the fabric of the simple dress she'd thrown into the luggage the night before. The lightweight cloth swirled around her knees, cascading from the empire waist like a waterfall. Taking a deep breath, she turned the latch on the door just enough to give Teddy access, then stepped back into the room to face him.

$$\infty\infty\infty$$

Teddy woke with a start and sat straight up in the unfamiliar bed. For one panicked moment, he thought he might have woken in Kate's bedroom. But no, the headboard behind his head looked like the one Sandra's Aunt Lou had given them around the time Danny was born. He reached over his head, feeling for the dent in the top corner of the solid mahogany, the dimple he'd caused by accident trying to move the heavy thing into their tiny bedroom. He looked around him, at the enormous room that seemed to engulf the bed and nightstand Sandra had placed in it.

What had possessed him to take Bob Wilson up on his offer and move into this giant of a house in the first place? Teddy felt sure there were rooms neither he nor Sandra had stepped into for the many months they'd been living there. He realized with a start that he had actively sought to isolate himself from her, a job made easier by the square footage of this place.

He glanced at his phone, dead. No need for a charger in a guest bedroom. Getting up from the bed, he felt sore and sticky, in great need of a shower. He knew he'd slept late into the day. He could tell from the light pouring in through the windows. If Sandra wasn't in the bedroom, he'd wait until after the shower to confront her.

The master bedroom door stood wide open, revealing a pristine bed. He sighed with relief and stepped into the bath. As the minutes passed by, he began rehearsing his words. The longer he thought about it, the more he came to feel put upon. He hadn't done anything really, not in the grand scheme of things.

When he headed downstairs, his indignation grew, feeling like a hot ball of fire in his chest. He looked for Sandra everywhere. When her phone went straight to voice mail and even showed as offline on the finder app, he called the church. As hours ticked by, and still he heard nothing, he even called his son. Indignation turned into worry, which sat in his gut, tumbling over and over until it felt red hot.

So, by the time he finally stood in front of Sandra's hotel room door, he had to take a deep breath before he could bring himself to knock and not bang his way in. He heard the lock click and turned the door handle. Stepping into the room, he felt suddenly underdressed in the pair of gray sweats and sloppy university t-shirt he'd been wearing the length of this tedious day.

Standing away from him with her arms loose by her sides, she fidgeted slightly, looking as if at any moment she might fly past him. He couldn't let that happen. The consequences to his career and his plans for the church would be devastating. Pushing his hands through his disheveled hair, he relaxed with effort.

"Sandra, you need to be reasonable about this. I would never do anything to hurt you."

"Really?" she cocked her head and turned to the little desk the room provided, placing her earrings on with a deft sort of savagery as she stared at him in the mirror. "It certainly feels like hurt." She turned, looking him straight in the eyes and jabbing at her sternum with her thumb. "Here, right here."

Then

Teddy fidgeted in the chair, watching Sandra dig into the taco plate she'd ordered, feeling a bead of sweat slide down his back. He knew asking her to marry him meant more than either one of them could conceive. As a minister, he willingly chose to live as a servant. Any woman agreeing to become his wife would also be expected to fulfill a certain role, a job in and of itself.

She paused, a taco dangling halfway between her mouth and plate. "Is something the matter?"

Caught up in his thoughts, Teddy took a moment to respond, and even then all he could manage was "what?"

She gestured to the food in front of him, "You haven't touched your food."

He smiled rather sheepishly and carefully picked up the closest shell, filled to the brim with taco meat, cheese, lettuce and tomatoes. He took a tender bite without tasting anything and forced a smile to his lips as if to say, *see, Sandra, I'm being good.*

She sat down her taco, shoving her plate to the side, laying her hands palm up on the table and wiggling her fingers in invitation. Teddy immediately did the same, taking hold of her hands, letting her warmth seep into his skin like a balm.

"You worried about your finals?" she asked.

Teddy shook his head. He was in his first year of seminary and doing well. "Sandra, I think you're the most interesting, thoughtful person I've ever met."

She smiled, sending more warmth coursing through his body. "I like you, too."

He grinned back at her because he couldn't help himself. "I never deserved someone like you," he started again.

"Are you trying to break up with me?" she blurted, turning pale.

Taking her reaction as a good sign, he swallowed, then continued, "I love you so much, I can't think of living my life without you."

"Yes."

"What?"

She wiggled in her seat. "You are asking me to marry you?"

Teddy felt his shoulders relax, but he forced himself to say, "The life I'm asking you to lead, being a preacher's wife, won't be easy, Sandra. There'll be plenty of times when the needs of the congregation may outweigh the needs of the family. I may not always have time for you, and much will be asked of you as well."

"But you think I can do it, don't you?"

"Of course," he assured her, "but I need you to make sure you want to do it before you agree to it."

"Yes," she said.

He shook her hands lightly. "I'm serious, Sandra. Think about it before you answer."

"Don't you know I've been thinking about it since the first time you came into the coffee shop and ordered a *plain, strong cup of coffee, miss*?" She pulled her hands out of his loose grasp and folded them in front of her chest. "You're sure you want to do this, Teddy?" she challenged.

"Yes, I'm sure," he retorted, sitting back. For a moment, they sat glaring at each other, their breaths quick. He thought for a moment he even saw her nostrils flare. Finally, he began to chuckle. "Well, I guess I should know you're perfectly capable of taking care of yourself."

"Darn right," she agreed.

He grinned at her stupidly for several minutes. They let the silence settle down around them, comfortable and sweet. Then, Sandra quirked her eyebrow at him, asking sweetly, "So, don't I get an engagement ring?"

∞ ∞ ∞

"Stop fidgeting," Lizzie's voice ordered from somewhere behind the voluminous layers of material making up her wedding dress. "What made you agree to wear this archaic dress? It's so much."

Sandra shrugged. "Teddy's mother had such a hopeful look when she asked me about it. How could I say no?"

"You'd better get used to saying no, Sandra," Lizzie tutted. "If you don't, you'll never have a life."

Sandra swallowed. Lizzie had just given voice to one of Sandra's nagging fears. "There's got to be a way to help other people without losing yourself completely," she said. "People in service do it all the time."

Lizzie turned Sandra so that they were facing each other. "If you have any doubts, now's the time to back out of this," she said, her face as serious as Sandra had ever seen.

"There are a hundred people out there," she sputtered. "Of course, I'm not going to call anything off."

Lizzie took Sandra's face in her hands and gave her a little shake. "Better to disappoint a hundred people now than to make the biggest mistake of your life."

"But I love Teddy," Sandra exclaimed, even though her thoughts had given way now and again, reflecting exactly what Lizzie was talking about.

"You're not just marrying Teddy, though," Lizzie persisted. "You're marrying into a whole new way of life, one you can't possibly conceive, even with that fertile imagination of yours."

"We've talked about this," Sandra protested, picking at the fabric of the scratchy dress Teddy's great-grandmother had worn, the one his mother had stored in the trunk at the foot of her bed, dragging it all across the country, even after it became apparent she would never have a daughter to wear it. "I know what I'm getting into."

Lizzie's eyes continued to pierce for several moments before she finally shrugged. "If that's how you really feel. Turn around now and let me finish with these tiny buttons. I think a Sadist designed this thing."

Sandra caught Lizzie's gaze in the mirror. "He loves me, Lizzie. He'll do anything for me."

The words came out forced, as if Sandra were trying to convince herself as much as her bridesmaid.

"What's taking you girls so long in here?" Sandra's mother said from the doorway. She had just finished with the hair and makeup team she had hired for the day, and she looked stunning.

Sandra glanced back at herself in the mirror, trying hard not to make any comparisons. She'd always had too much of her father in her when it came to the looks department. Her mother glided across the room, blocking Sandra's view in the mirror as she laid her fingers on her daughter's shoulders. She looked up and down the dress Sandra wore and tutted.

"I can't believe I couldn't talk you out of this hideous

dress," she leaned in to whisper in Sandra's ear, ever the proper person, not wanting anyone to hear her complaint. Her mother's breath was hot against her skin and smelled like the cheap champagne father's boss at the paper company had supplied for the occasion.

Her mother had not understood Sandra's choice to marry a future minister, either, wanting to know more than once why Sandra had not managed to nab a future doctor or lawyer. Hadn't they sent her to a four-year university instead of community college for just that purpose?

Sandra pulled back to look at her mother closely. Underneath the makeup that made her mother look like a cover model, Sandra could see the lines around her mother's eyes and mouth that no makeup could disguise. If Sandra couldn't convince her own mother to accept Jesus as Lord, how did she expect to succeed as Teddy's wife?

Pushing the niggling questions out of her mind with some effort, Sandra straightened her shoulders and managed through tightened lips, "I don't mind it, Mother."

Looking back at her as if she could read everything in Sandra's mind, all her doubts and fears and dreams, too, her mother smiled crookedly and shook her head. "You always did think better of people than they deserved, my little butterball," she quipped, using the pet name from Sandra's childhood and pinching her daughter's cheek with more force than necessary.

She turned on her heel and left the room, throwing over her shoulder as she went, "Hurry now. They have another ceremony at 2, and everyone is waiting."

Sandra stood watching the door after her mother left, unable to move. She listened to her ragged breaths move in and out of her body, sounding like a rasp against rusty metal. She felt Lizzie's fingers, warm and re-assuring, wrap around her own and squeeze.

"You're not making a mistake, Sandra. You can do this. And Teddy will never fail you," she said, giving Sandra's hand a little shake.

"No," Sandra said on a shaky breath, "Teddy will do his best to love me, but only God never fails. If I can remember that, I'll have everything I ever need. "

"Spoken like a true preacher's wife," Lizzie agreed. She motioned to the door. "Now, let's get you married."

Now

Teddy glanced at Sandra, realizing with a start he hadn't really looked at her in a long time, too long. Even with the obvious effort she'd put into her current appearance, he could see the lines around her eyes and mouth, the testament to her years spent taking care of other people as much as she cared for Danny and himself. The thought caused another stab of guilt to slice through him. He pushed it aside as just so much jumbled thinking.

Looking down at his own clothes, he grimaced at the round-the-house sweats and t-shirt that seemed careless now, as if Sandra weren't worth the effort. He hadn't even bothered to shave, or better yet, bring her flowers. He stepped further into the room and sat on the bed, shoving his fingers through his hair, then resting his head in his hands.

"I didn't mean to hurt you," he admitted finally, his voice coming out pitched, like a naughty child.

A little click sounded at the back of Sandra's throat. "You still don't believe you've done anything wrong," she exclaimed. He looked up to see her shaking her head. She always seemed to know him better than he knew himself. "Please go," she breathed out.

"Now, see here," he barked, his voice rising indignantly. He bit his lower lip to stop himself from saying more and tasted blood. "Please," he started again, "may we talk about this?"

Her shoulders fell, and she moved to sit down in the room's only chair. Smoothing her skirt with her hands, she rested her fingers on her knees and took a deep breath. When she shifted her eyes to look at him, Teddy felt a sharp jolt up and down his spine, like a bucket of cold water pouring over his head. But the next second, his pride stiffened his resolve. Surely, Sandra was over-reacting to this whole situation.

"You're the one who never wanted to come to the gym, who refuses to support my dreams for our church," the words came out in a pant. To his horror, he finished by crying out in a petulant voice, "What did you expect me to do?"

She blinked at him. "The devil's in you, Teddy Pike," she said, her voice soft, without any heat. Then, more to herself or even God than to him, "What are we going to do?"

The devil in him?!! "That's just ridiculous. We just have to learn to communicate better," he argued.

"You mean I need to learn to just go along with whatever you decide to do?" She shook her head. "I don't think so."

"This was a mistake," Teddy muttered. "I should have given you more time to cool off and come to your senses."

"Oh, this was a mistake?" she stood, her hands on her hips. "I like how easily you can find fault in yourself when it comes to me. You can't see the end of your nose to spite your face." She walked over to the door and opened it. "Go," she ordered, no polite *please* this time.

Teddy walked past her, trying not to notice how she flinched away from him as he went. "This isn't finished," he warned.

"Find Kate somewhere else to work and part ways with her, and maybe we can talk again," she said through tight lips.

Before he could respond to that, she shut the door on him, leaving him standing in the hall, his mouth open in shock. He knew one thing. Kate was the best assistant he had ever had. He wasn't about to lose her. Sandra would calm down. Teddy hadn't done anything unthinkable. He felt better by the time he'd reached the lobby.

Yes, this would all blow over in a week or two. Every marriage hit little bumps like this. He'd counseled too many couples through similar hard times. Teddy even managed to whistle as he jogged across the parking lot to his vehicle, letting the engine idle for a long moment before pulling out on the road.

Sandra's fingers tightened on the wheel as her car neared the church. If it weren't for the women's conference, she'd probably disappear for a while, running away from her current reality. She shook her head slightly to stop that kind of thinking. She owed it to herself and to Teddy to fight for her marriage, to remind Teddy about his duty to her and to God. No, duty wasn't the right word. Teddy had loved her once, more than anyone except his love for God. Now, he seemed to have forgotten about his feelings for either of them.

But Sandra realized that fixing her relationship with Teddy was going to take some serious work as she passed his office on the way to her room. There he sat at his big desk, the door between his and Kate's offices wide open, and the younger woman draped over him as he worked.

"That won't do at all," Mike Bradley's deep voice said from behind her.

Sandra started, turning to look up and up to the tall man's face. His strong jaw tensed as he looked down at Sandra. She tried not to blush as she felt herself and her marital problems exposed. She might as well be standing in the hallway stripped naked, she thought.

He took one step toward Teddy's office, but Sandra reached out her hand to stop him. "It's the church's business as much as it's yours," he explained, his eyes full of sympathy and apology all at once.

"Please, can we give him a chance to snap out of it?" she pleaded.

But at that moment, Kate laughed prettily, rubbing her hand up and down Teddy's chest. The intimacy of the motion turned Sandra's stomach.

"I don't think so, Sandra," Mike told her. He took her gently by the elbow and guided her right into Teddy's office.

Sandra paled as Kate and then Teddy looked up at them. For a long, agonizing moment, no one moved. Then, Teddy seemed to come to himself. He stood, breaking contact with Kate, and shoved his hands in his pockets, looking like a defiant child.

"Did you arrange this?" Teddy blurted, breaking the awkward silence with an awkwardness all its own.

Mike reached behind him and closed the office door, shutting them off from any prying eyes. "Sandra didn't need to arrange anything, Theodore," he said, his voice sharp. "You two are on display for the whole church to see."

"Don't be ridiculous," Kate exclaimed, her fingers splaying across her hips.

Even Teddy looked at the younger woman in a bit of shock then. "Maybe you should go get some coffee," he suggested.

Mike's jaw set. "Yes," he agreed, "perhaps she should."

Kate patted Teddy's shoulder and just stopped herself from smoothing his hair before leaving the office with as much dignity as a 28-year-old could muster. If the situation weren't imploding her life, Sandra might have mustered the energy to see the amusement in it.

The door closed again once Kate left the room, and Sandra,

zapped of strength suddenly, sank into one of the visitor chairs in front of her husband's desk. Was it a good sign she could still think of him as hers?

Mike stayed on his feet, towering over her, even blocking the office light. Teddy obviously felt intimidated. He stood up taller, taking his hands out of his pockets. They lay in tight fists along the sides of his thighs. Mike sighed.

"I'll find a new place for Kate to work, somewhere in town," he said, turning to Sandra. "You can pick a new assistant for Teddy," he told her.

"Now see here," Teddy exclaimed. "You can't decide what happens in my church without me."

Mike's brow rose. He continued holding Sandra's gaze, even though his next words were directed at Teddy. "Your church?" he asked. "I thought this body of believers belonged to God?"

A heavy silence descended. Sandra, unable to deal with the tension, picked at the corner of the purse sitting on her lap. Mike finally moved to the other visitor chair and sank into it.

"I know you don't want to hear this," he said, "but somebody needs to tell you that your actions are putting your ministry in jeopardy." When Teddy didn't respond, Mike added, "Unless you want me to call a meeting of the deacons to discuss your actions."

Teddy huffed, "I've had enough problems with them lately."

"When did you stop loving God?" Sandra asked, looking up at him past the sheen of tears in her eyes.

"You have to know this behavior is out of character for you, Teddy," Mike added.

She watched as Teddy looked between his two interrogators. A bead of angry sweat rolled down the side of his head and plopped on the shoulder of his crisp shirt, making a misshapen blob there. For one crazy moment, Sandra hoped this would be it, the moment Teddy came back to her. But instead, he dashed all her hopes.

"I've done nothing wrong," he repeated, with that gleam in his eye telling Sandra he had dug in.

"What are we going to do?" she said to no one in particular, and her tears really began to fall then, fast and hot, nothing she could do would stop them.

∞ ∞ ∞

Teddy's face flamed red. He could feel the heat surge through his body, even though not even the muscles in his eyelids twitched. Was he angry, embarrassed, ashamed, watching Sandra cry like that? The only thing keeping Teddy in his chair was Mike's watchful eyes on him. That man had the power to make or break Teddy's plans. How little Teddy liked admitting that.

A moment later, perhaps a moment too late, Teddy rose to stand in front of Sandra's chair. They'd been together almost 30 years, and he wasn't a monster, after all. He reached down to cup her wet cheek in his palm, regardless of Mike's stare, only to have Sandra jerk away from him as if his touch burned.

"You don't have the right to comfort me," she panted, yanking a tissue from the bag in her lap. "Not when you're the author of my misery."

Mike cleared his throat. "I'm no counselor," he said into the quiet, "but it's clear some sort of intervention would do you both some good." He rose to his considerable height, yanking at his collar uncomfortably. "I'll be bringing this matter up to the deacons, Teddy," he said. "In the meantime, I suggest you work on mending fences with your wife."

Before Teddy, still in shock at Sandra's rejection, could respond to Mike's threat, the other man strode out of the office, closing the door behind him as he went. Teddy sat back on his desk, crossing his arms in front of his chest. He had to admit to a kind of stinging pain somewhere deep in his thorax that didn't want to go away. Still, his pride got the better of him.

"You're not some saint," he blurted before he could stop himself. "You're every bit to blame the way you've been sulking around ever since Danny graduated and moved out of the house for good," he heard himself continue. *Why couldn't he just shut up?*

But Sandra surprised him. Instead of arguing, she took a deep breath and rose from her chair. "Will you agree to quit seeing Kate and to getting some marriage counseling with me?" she asked so quietly, he had to strain to hear her.

Teddy stood, too, which brought him within an inch of his wife. He realized with a start, it just might be the closest he'd come to her in a good, long while. Still, he couldn't stop himself.

"I told you, nothing's happened with Kate," he exclaimed.

Sandra blinked back another onslaught of tears before looking up at him. Her eyes were dull and so sad, shockingly lifeless when she always had the fire to motivate, especially himself. "Then, let's make sure nothing happens," she said, then paused before asking, "You do want to stay married to me?"

Something clutched at the pit of Teddy's stomach. How could she ask such a question? Had he really been such a terrible husband?

Love her as I love the church, Theodore, another voice told him.

Don't I love Your church, LORD, he thought. Haven't I given my life to it?

He looked up to see Sandra turning away from him, reaching for the doorknob to his office door. He realized with a horrified start that he hadn't answered her question. Worse yet, had he not just seconds before dug in to argue with God?

Before she could leave him, Teddy leaped ahead of her, placing his back against the door, blocking her way. His eyes slid to her face. Her face. *Oh, Jesus,* he prayed, *have I caused that misery I see in the eyes of my one and only, flesh of my flesh?*

He didn't need to wait for an answer before sliding to his knees, taking Sandra's hands in his own. He laid his forehead against her fingers and breathed her in, the familiar scent that was hers alone.

"I want you, Sandra," he finally managed. "I'm sorry that I made you doubt that."

She cocked her head. "It's not that easy. We have some work to do to fix us."

"All right," he agreed past the lump in his throat. Certain images were flashing across his mind, memories of his actions these last few weeks.

Suddenly, he remembered something else, too. That first little church he officially pastored, just himself and Sandra and a couple hundred faithful congregants. They celebrated the presence of Jesus in that LORD'S house. It had been some time since he'd felt that kind of joy in His presence.

"I have some work to do with God, too," he told Sandra, cupping her face in his hands as he stood. "What have I done, Sandra?"

She squeezed his hands with her own, and he thought her face looked lighter. "It wasn't just you," she said. "It takes two people to make or break a marriage. Isn't that what we always say?"

No wonder he loved her, Teddy thought. And then, he held his hands up between them, an offering. "Will you pray with me, wife?"

She took his hands instantly, breathing a long sigh. Teddy bowed his head, but a smile played at his lips. Thankfully, God's forgiveness covered even an older man's foolishness. Only Jesus truly understood our need for second chances, He who needed no second chance but took the punishment for all the sins in the world, including Teddy's own.

Books By This Author

Thicker Than Blood

A young woman looking to re-build her future gets caught up in a decades-old mystery.

Her Unbroken Heart

Beatrice Jones has everything she ever wanted in her career as a cardio-thoracic surgeon. She left home at 18 and never looked back. Until now.

Sent back home to perform a risky surgery, Beatrice comes face-to-face with the family who never wanted her. The life she has collides with the life that might have been, especially when she discovers that Jude Newman, the boy who loved her once, still looks at her and sees the girl he wanted to marry.

Does Beatrice want to stay trapped in her successful, albeit lonely, career, or can she find a way through forgiveness to look beyond the past and embrace a different future?

His Forever Home

Finn and Mellie were destined to be together--until life got in the way. After twenty years apart, the two get a second chance to find each other. Will a mystery from way back when rise up to keep them apart for good, or will they find a way to be together? A story about forgiving each other--and ourselves.

A Love Of Her Own

Bess Taylor has a problem, but really that is nothing new. Married for only six months, she's already a widow thanks to the war in Vietnam. She could go on living as before, sharing a small apartment with three other hard-working women, belonging to no one and having next to nothing.

The problem is, Bess' soldier husband left her with a legacy, a tiny baby growing under Bess' lonely heart.

Seeking the support she needs to bring a child into the world, Bess goes to her late husband's family. His brother Judd, a cowboy and the local sheriff, has a black stare that seems to see right through Bess, right down to her darkest, best-kept secrets. Agnes, her mother-in-law, is a different story. That woman's kind nature and loving personality convince Bess to stay.

Just when Bess thinks she might finally make a home for herself with the Taylors, the kind of home she never had growing up as an orphan, a dark figure from her past looms up to threaten the fragile peace Bess has discovered.

Will her past force Bess to run away from the closest thing to family she has ever known, or will she finally find what her lonely heart has always sought--a love of her own?

Fire In The Bones

Neely Watts has come to the Jessup Ranch in search of answers. Twelve years after being dumped at the altar and regardless of her success as a country singer, Neely has a hole in her heart that nothing, not even fame and fortune, seems to fill.

When Neely returns to her Texas roots hoping to find a

happiness that has eluded her ever since that fateful day when Tom Rice gave his name to another girl, the last thing she expects to discover is her need for a relationship with God.

But before she comes to truly understand the importance knowing God plays in her life, Neely also has to come to terms with her past. Tom Rice, now a widower, offers Neely a second chance at the life she should have had, if she can forgive him for breaking her heart. And then, there is Antonio Ramos, a successful neurosurgeon who makes Neely see herself in a new light.

And quietly, in the background, Mordecai Jessup offers Neely the one thing she doesn't even realize she's been missing, a relationship with her Savior Christ, upon Whose promises alone Neely can truly depend.

The Texas Stray: Only God Could Lead Her Home (Book 1)

A girl gives up a dream proposal to pursue her dream career. Will her dreamy boss keep her from the boy back home?

Camden Meets His Match (The Texas Stray: Book 2)

Brenda Camden made one mistake that cost her the marriage to her true love. Now, 7 years later, will her strong, independent ex-husband find the way back to her, or will Brenda need to finally define who she is without him? As Brenda turns to God in her search for answers, she struggles to forgive herself and wonders how the stubborn, handsome man she married can learn to love her again. Will God help her find the path that will make her family whole?

Macy's Treasure

What happens when a shy bookworm gets paired with the handsome star of the high school football team, who just happens to be the boy next door?

Gathering Flint At Claremore Mound

A collection of poems, reflecting my western roots.

Discover

Visit my author website for more information, the latest updates and blog posts:

https://www.RamonaLevacy.com

Visit my day job, where I educate consumers about health topics and help run our family-owned supplement store. Find my health blogs, podcasts and more:

http://www.betsyhealth.com

Acknowledgement

Thank you, my readers, for taking the time to hopefully enjoy my novels. If it weren't for you, what would I do with all these words and stories, waiting to be shared?

I truly feel that God has called me to use my writing to spread the good news of His love for us. Ever since I learned how to write, I have wanted to be an author. I am so thankful that online publishing came along (and you wonderful readers with it) so that I could make my dream a reality.

As life grows ever-more challenging, I find solace in hoping that I might share the lessons I've learned (having practiced hard faith) with you. Through my blog posts, novels, and hopefully a useful devotional some time in the future, I am moving forward, trusting that God will use the words He has given me to help someone, somewhere, at just the right time.

If this collection of novellas was just the right someone and somewhere for you, could you let me know? I appreciate any encouragement we can share. Write me at: ramonalevacy@ramonalevacy.com.